Long Way Home

TANISHA STEWART

I0662727

Long Way Home
Copyright © 2024 Tanisha Stewart

All rights reserved.

Long Way Home is a work of fiction. Any resemblance to events, locations, or persons living or dead is coincidental. No part of this book may be reproduced in any written, electronic, recording, or photocopying form without written permission of the author, Tanisha Stewart.

Books may be purchased in quantity and for special sales by contacting the publisher, Tanisha Stewart, at tanishastewart.author@gmail.com.

First Edition
Published in the United States of America
by Tanisha Stewart

Shout Outs

I have three special shout outs for this read:

The first is my editor, Cady Anne of Cynful Monarch. She always comes through in a clutch with edits for my stories to help make them shine in the best way they can.

PS: She is also an author – check out her catalog under Cyn on Amazon!

The second shout out is for author J.R. Mason for her murderous threats after beta reading this book. She thoroughly cursed me out to make this story better! Lol Check out her books and get lost in the Stolen Pieces series. Trust me; you won't regret it!

Last, but not least, I would like to thank my ARC Team. When I reached out, each of you immediately stepped up to the plate to read this story and help spread it to the world. Thank you :)

Table of Contents

Long Way Home

Chapter 1

I rushed through the mall to Farley's Clothing Store, fingers scrunched around the strap of my purse as it threatened to bounce off my shoulder. My son Benji's hand was tightly gripped in my other hand. The mall was a symphony of distractions: children's laughter mingling with the sharp scent of cinnamon pretzels and neon signs flashing sales above the heads of a sea of shoppers.

I totally spaced on grabbing a gift for Peter's seventh birthday. This was horrible for two reasons: First, Peter was Benji's best friend, and secondly, he was my godson.

Clara, Peter's mother, was my best friend and Benji's godmother. My son had celebrated his seventh birthday last month and Clara had gone all out with gifts.

I wasn't a terrible godmother - I helped pay for Peter's party and hired the clown. Clara had done much of the same for me with Benji's birthday.

"Mommy! Can I go on the rides?" Benji asked, his tiny legs fighting to keep up with my generous strides.

I hesitated, knowing the bustling mall was no place for a child to be alone. But Peter's party was starting in an hour, and I had no gift. Plus the ride was directly in front of the store so I would be able to see him at all times, and besides, if I didn't let him go on the rides, Benji would be whining in my ear the whole time we shopped for Peter's gift. I didn't want the headache when

I would be in and out of the store in less than five minutes. I already had in mind what I was getting for Peter – a few cute outfits. "Just two minutes," I told myself, trying to quell the rising worry.

He immediately lit up when I told him he could go on the ride, and at first I was going to take it back, but then I considered once again that I would only be a few minutes in the store, plus I already said no earlier when he begged for a pretzel. My stomach grumbled at that moment. I should have given in to the damn pretzel because I had barely eaten anything since Benji and I shared breakfast out on our back patio this morning. The mouthwatering scent of garlic parmesan filled my memories and I almost told Benji we were going back to get pretzels, but I snapped out of it, remembering that we didn't have much time. We could get pretzels on the way out. Benji always opted for the sweet kind with cinnamon and icing all over the top. My lips quirked into a soft smile at the thought while Benji continued to beam up at me, eagerly awaiting his chance to get on his beloved mall ride.

I dropped my son's hand and grabbed some change out of my wallet. Several quarters tumbled into Benji's excited palm. "Stay on the rides until I come out," I instructed. "Do you know how to work them?"

Benji was already rushing over to put quarters in the slot. The ride he selected was a fancy red convertible that bounced up and down and swerved back and forth as if it were traveling down a road. It also had a black plastic wheel that turned so the child could feel like they were controlling the vehicle. It was cute but ridiculous in my opinion because although the car bounced and swerved, it didn't actually go anywhere.

Oh well. At least he will be occupied for a few minutes.

I watched my son's glee-filled expression for a few moments then hurried into the store to grab the outfits for Peter. As I perused the pants section, I kept one eye on Benji, who was doing exactly as I instructed - staying on the ride - and the other on the price tags.

I wanted to get some nice outfits for my godson, but my income as a freelance writer for an online magazine wouldn't exactly allow me to splurge. The crowd outside the store thickened, a tidal wave of shoppers that seemed to swallow Benji in their midst. I craned my neck, but the harsh glare of the overhead lights turned the sea of heads into a blur of shadows. Then I saw Benji's head through the sea of people who were passing the store and he was still on the ride. I relaxed.

A thought jolted me - I needed to submit my latest article to Dexter, my boss. I calculated how much time the party would probably take and whether I could swing a few hours on my computer before collapsing from exhaustion.

The article needed to be in by midnight if I had any chance of being published in the next release of the magazine.

I refocused and grabbed a few cute outfits I had never seen Peter wear before, then headed to the register. Once I got there, I realized I almost forgot about my son. I turned back to look at the ride, standing on my tiptoes and craning my neck, but he wasn't on it anymore.

My heart fluttered as the line before me moved forward. There was one more lady, then it would be my turn to cash out.

Where was my son?

An older gentleman came to the line to stand behind me. He stared me up and down as I peered around him, continuing to scan the area around the rides. I didn't see Benji. *Damn it, Benji!* I didn't want to lose my place in line, but it looked like I was about to.

"Are you okay, Miss?" he asked, at the exact moment I stepped out of line to look for my son.

"Benji!" I called, rushing toward the entrance of the store while glancing in every direction to figure out where he wandered off to. "Benji!"

"Right here, Mommy!"

Benji materialized seemingly out of nowhere, holding an ice cream cone topped with fudge.

My heartrate calmed.

"Where did you go?" I asked, though it was obvious now that I spotted the ice cream stand that was a short distance away. It was around the corner from Farley's Clothing Store, so that was why I hadn't immediately located my son.

Where the hell did he get money for ice cream? I only gave him a few quarters for the car ride, so Benji wouldn't have had enough to buy one of his own. Unless the ice cream man gave it to him for free. I stared at the stand and the man smiled and waved at me, but I gave him a side eye. I always taught my son not to talk to strangers, but this man was undoing my work by offering my child ice cream. It was a nice gesture, yes, but in today's times, you could never be too careful. Stories every day arose about child predators, and they often lured kids with things they liked: candy, toys, dogs, the list went on and on. I glowered at the ice cream man once again and he turned up his nose at me before focusing on his next customer.

Benji looked at the floor, then up at me with puppy-dog eyes as he pointed. "Daddy bought me ice cream."

My heart lurched, then sank as I stared at my son.

He couldn't have possibly thought the ice cream man was his father, could he? They looked nothing alike – the man was Caucasian while Roman, Benji's father, was Black. A wave of sadness passed through me as I thought of the fact that my son seemed to be getting worse.

Tears threatened to assemble at the corners of my eyes, but I blinked them away. Benji's father was a touchy subject but as many times as I tried to lovingly tell my son it wasn't possible for him to be seeing his father anywhere, much less for him to buy him ice cream, it always went in one ear and out the other.

Part of me wondered if Benji might be suffering from a psychological disorder. Benji had already been seeing a therapist since his father's tragic passing, but maybe I needed to increase the frequency of his appointments. Or maybe I should have taken Benji to see someone else, especially since his claims of seeing his father became more frequent in recent times. But another side of me held back, crippled by the weight of what it could possibly mean.

I knelt to face him, speaking softly at first. "What did I tell you about wandering off? Didn't I say to stay on the ride?"

His face fell. "Yes," he said in a voice barely above a whisper. "But Daddy..."

Something snapped within me. "Give me the cone," I demanded. I hadn't meant for my words to come out harshly, but they did. Besides what may be going on in my son's mind, he needed to know it wasn't safe to wander off, much less accept food from strangers.

"Mommy!" He whined, but I wasn't trying to hear that.

His fingers gripped the cone tighter.

"Give it to me now, Benji."

As I wrenched the ice cream cone from Benji's hand, memories flooded back of the day he'd wandered off at the park, the sheer panic of not finding him for those endless minutes. "Safety first," I whispered, more to myself than to him. Taking a few steps toward a nearby trash can to throw it away, I immediately caused the store alarms to go off.

My entire body was hot with embarrassment. Peter's outfits were still cradled under my left arm. So much for teaching my son a lesson, but I held my head high as I threw the ice cream cone in the trash, firmly grabbed Benji's hand, and led him back into the store to pay for Peter's clothes.

A few other customers glared at me as I walked past them, but I pretended not to care. It wasn't like I was planning to steal merchandise. It was a simple mistake.

Benji wasn't making the situation any better. He was still crying as we stood in line behind the older gentleman who was originally behind me.

When Benji sank to the floor like he was about to throw a tantrum, I gently but firmly yanked him back up, kneeling once again so we were eye-level. "You will not have a fit in this store, you hear me? You know what I told you. If you keep on crying, we will go straight home and I will drop Peter's gift off to him tomorrow."

The older gentleman from before glanced over his shoulder at us after inserting his card into the reader. "Everything okay, Miss?" he asked with a tone of concern.

"We're fine."

Benji immediately straightened up.

The older gentleman exited the store and I approached the counter.

I quickly paid for my items then led Benji out of the store and mall. He kept craning his neck to look back at the ice cream stand, but I urged him forward. Part of me wanted to get him another cone, but the other part knew I had to be firm in my discipline.

Relief flooded my veins when we exited the mall out to the bright and sunny parking lot.

Benji was back to normal as we walked through the parking lot to find my minivan.

There weren't too many cars around us, despite today being a Saturday. The inside of the mall was very busy, but the number of cars outside didn't reflect it. Maybe everyone else parked at different entrances. Or maybe I saw the crowd as bigger than it actually was because I was in a rush.

I sighed and clicked my key fob, opening the rear passenger's seat first to put Benji in his booster seat. Though he was seven years old, my son was still small for his age, so I wouldn't transition him to a regular seat for at least another year. After I clicked the straps together, the thought crossed my mind that I should have bought one of those huge gift bags for Peter's clothes too. Maybe I would pick one up at the drugstore on the way to Clara's house.

Once my son was secure, I popped the trunk. After slamming it shut, I noticed swift movement on my right side.

Pain erupted in the back of my head and everything went black.

Chapter 2

Darkness surrounded me as I came to. The back of my head was searing with pain. Vomit rose to my throat and before I could reach for a wastebasket, it escaped my lips.

"Oh my God..." I said after I finished heaving my insides all over myself. The sharp smell of bile mixed with the sterile hospital air.

"Oh dear, let's get you cleaned up," a nearby voice said. Through hazy vision, I heard the squeak of rubber-soled shoes approaching. Gentle hands helped me sit up in what felt like a hospital bed, its metal rails cold against my skin. A steady beeping somewhere to my left matched my quickening pulse.

"Ma'am? Can you see me?" the soft feminine voice asked.

I shook my head, instantly regretting the movement as pain shot through my skull. The fluorescent lights above were visible, but everything else was a blur of shadows and shapes.

I held a shaky hand in front of my face, seeing only a darker smudge against the hazy background. "Oh my God..." I repeated, my voice barely a whisper. "Where am I? Why can't I see anything?"

"You're at Clearview Hospital," the woman said in a soft tone. "I'm your nurse, Martha. I'll get the doctor to

8

discuss your condition." She paused, and I heard the rustle of her scrubs as she shifted. "The police officers outside would like to speak with you when you're ready."

Police officers? My chest tightened. *Why would...* Then it hit me, the memory slamming into me like a physical blow. "Where's Benji?" The words came out in a panic.

"Ma'am?"

"My son, Benji! Where is he?" My voice cracked.

The silence that followed seemed to stretch forever. The beeping of my heart monitor grew faster, more insistent.

"Ma'am," Martha said carefully, "we weren't aware there was a child with you when you were found. We..."

Fragments of memory flashed through my mind: Benji laughing on the mall ride, his small hand in mine, strapping him into his booster seat, the flash of movement behind me... My trembling hand reached toward the back of my throbbing head, finding only layers of gauze wrapped like a turban.

"What happened to me?" I cried out, cutting Martha off. "Where is my son?"

She grabbed my wrists, her hands warm but firm. "Ma'am, please try to stay calm. Let's get you cleaned up first, then—"

"I don't give a damn about that. Where is Benji?"

From the doorway came the sound of a throat clearing. "Good evening," a male voice said, his professional tone carefully measured. "I'm Doctor Roberts. I'm glad to see that you're awake! I just have a few questions for you."

Through my blurred vision, I could make out his white coat as he approached. Beyond him, through the open door, I glimpsed what looked like two uniformed figures standing guard.

The doctor asked me a bunch of questions as he examined me, but I didn't care about those questions - where was my son?

Voices in the hallway grew louder – familiar voices. The quick tap of heels against linoleum preceded my friends' arrival.

"Nadine!" Clara's voice broke on my name.

I turned toward the sound, my vision finally clear enough to see my bestie, Clara. At first, I wondered, *How did she know I was here?* But then I remembered that Clara was my emergency contact for all things since I wasn't married and my parents were deceased. My other bestie Angelique's mascara-streaked face scrunched with concern as she rushed to my bedside. Their arms encircled me, careful to avoid the IV lines and monitors.

Only then, surrounded by the warmth of my friends, did I let myself break. My sobs echoed off the sterile walls as the reality of my situation crashed over me – Benji was gone.

When I told my friends my son was missing, the same panic I felt crossed their terrified features. "Oh my God..." Clara said. "Nadine, if I had known... did no one think to check the backseat?"

We looked up at the doctor who still wore a neutral expression. I didn't know how he could be so calm, while my insides were going crazy. I understood it wasn't his son who was missing, but couldn't he show a bit more concern?

One of the officers stepped into the room. "Ma'am? Are you ready to answer a few questions?"

"No, I'm not ready to answer any questions!" I snapped. "The only question that needs to be answered is where is my son?"

The officer waited a beat before responding. "Ma'am, we weren't aware there was a child with you when you were found. A passerby found you in the parking lot and called us, and..."

"Did no one think to check the backseat?" I demanded, cutting off his explanation with impatience. "I strapped him into his booster seat right before I was hit in the back of the head. How could no one know my son was with me?"

The officer seemed to be at a loss for words, but his partner stepped forward. "Ma'am, I just called for one of our detectives. He's in the area so he will be here shortly."

"Good," I said, knowing I was being rude but not giving a damn about it. Something told me I was also being irrational by thinking people should automatically know my son was with me, but I brushed it away. My only concern was finding out where he had gone. Did he wander back into the mall looking for help? Was he still in the parking lot somewhere?

Then a shuddering thought hit me... Had someone taken him?

"Ms. Wilson?" A deep voice came from the doorway. Through my tears, I saw a tall man in a dark suit showing his badge. "I'm Detective Lane. I know this is difficult, but we need to ask you some questions about your son."

Clara squeezed my hand while Angelique dabbed at my face with a tissue. The heart monitor's beeping slowed as I forced myself to take deep breaths.

Doctor Roberts stepped forward. "Detective, my patient has suffered a severe concussion. Her temporary loss of vision is just now resolving, and she's still quite disoriented."

"I understand, Doctor," the detective said, his tone gentle but firm. "But we need to move quickly now that we know about the child." He turned to me. "Ms. Wilson, can you tell me the last thing you remember?"

I closed my eyes, trying to focus through the throbbing in my head. "We were at Briarwood Mall. Benji..." My voice caught. "Benji was playing on those mechanical rides while I shopped for Peter's birthday gift." The memory of picking out clothes for Clara's seven-year-old son, Benji's godbrother, seemed surreal now. "Then we left. I remember strapping him into his booster seat." The memory became fuzzy. "I was putting the shopping bags in the trunk, and then..." My hand instinctively went to the back of my head.

"What time was this?" Detective Lane asked, jotting notes in a small notebook.

"Around..." I glanced at Clara.

"It's six o'clock now," she supplied softly, her own voice shaking.

The weight of her words enveloped me like a dark cloud. It was six o'clock?

My breath caught in my throat, but I continued. "The mall... we left around three. Oh God, he's been missing for hours, and nobody even knew!" The monitor's beeping increased again.

"Ms. Wilson," Detective Lane said, pulling up a chair. "We need to call in an Amber Alert. In order to do that, I'm going to need some information from you about your son. The quicker we move, the faster we can find him." He scanned something on an iPad, then said, "Officer Rachel Patel will be your Family Liaison Officer. She'll be here shortly to help coordinate everything."

12

A female officer appeared in the doorway, tablet in hand. "Detective? The mall security footage is ready."

The detective stood. "I'll be right back, Ms. Wilson. Try to rest for a second and remember any other details you can."

"Rest for a second?" I wanted to ask, but Detective Lane was already out the door. How did he expect me to rest when he just told me they were about to call in an Amber Alert about my son?

Once he was out of the room, Clara gripped my hand tighter. "Tom is bringing Peter to the hospital," she said softly.

I was bewildered for a moment. Things were moving too fast for my brain to catch up to what was happening. Too many moving pieces – my head was spinning. A wave of dizziness passed through me, and I had to hold to the rails on the side of the bed and close my eyes as I waited for it to pass through me. Once it ended, I opened my eyes and turned to Clara, my vision sharpening more by the second. "Why would Tom bring Peter here?"

Clara swallowed. "He said he wanted to make sure you were good."

A tiny smile played at my lips but died before it had the chance to spread. I appreciated Tom's gesture, but I didn't think the hospital was the right place for my seven-year-old godson Peter to be. What was he going to do here with a sea of adults? I wanted to protest, but Clara already said they were on their way. I forced myself to relax.

Clara studied me. "We're here for you, Nadine. Whatever you need."

I nodded, my throat tight. Clara had always been more than just Peter's mother - she was the closest thing to family I had besides Benji. I had nobody else, but how could I face her knowing I'd failed to protect my son?

"The police will find him," Angelique said firmly, but I could hear the tremor in her voice.

Doctor Roberts cleared his throat. "I need to check your vitals again, Ms. Wilson. And then we should clean you up."

This time, I didn't argue. As Martha helped me out of the soiled hospital gown, I tried to focus on remembering every detail of those last moments in the parking lot. Somewhere in my damaged memory was a clue that might help find my son.

Once I was back in my hospital bed, Detective Lane returned with Officer Patel, a petite woman with kind eyes and an efficient manner. They pulled up chairs while Clara and Angelique stepped back, staying close but giving us space.

"Ms. Wilson," Officer Patel said, her voice steady and calm, "I'll be coordinating between you and our search teams. First, we need a detailed description of Benji and what he was wearing today."

I swallowed hard. "He's seven. Short hair cut, brown eyes like mine. He has a small birthmark shaped like a crescent moon behind his right ear." My voice cracked. "He was wearing his favorite blue dinosaur hoodie – dark blue with a red T-Rex. Khaki shorts, red sneakers with white laces."

"Any distinguishing features? Recent injuries, scars?"

"He scraped his knee last week climbing trees. It's still scabbed over." The mundane detail of treating his knee with Batman bandages and kisses made my chest ache.

Detective Lane looked up from his notebook. "We've reviewed some of the security footage. We can see you and Benji leaving the mall at 3:12 PM. The cameras show you both reaching your minivan, but then there's a blind spot where your vehicle was parked." He paused. "The next footage shows a dark van pulling away at 3:17 PM, but the angle doesn't give us the plate number."

My head throbbed as I tried to remember. "I don't... I can't remember seeing a van."

"That's okay," Officer Patel assured me. "With concussions, memory loss around the trauma is common. Sometimes the memories return gradually."

"We're pulling footage from other cameras in the area," Detective Lane added. "And we're getting the Amber Alert ready to broadcast. Do you have a recent photo of Benji?"

"My phone..." I looked around frantically.

"It was in your purse," Clara said, stepping forward. "The police have it for evidence, but I have dozens of photos of Benji on my phone. From the park last weekend." She pulled out her phone, quickly finding a clear, recent photo of my son's smiling face.

The sound of rapid footsteps in the hallway made us all look up. Tom, Clara's brother, appeared in the doorway with Peter clutching his hand. My eyes met Tom's for a moment, and I saw the barely contained worry in his expression. He opened his mouth as if to say something, then stopped himself.

"Tee Tee Nadine?" Peter's small voice trembled. "Where's Benji?"

Clara quickly moved to intercept them. "Peter, honey, let's go get some water while the police talk to Tee Tee."

As Clara led Peter away, and Angelique followed, Tom lingered in the doorway, his presence both comforting and unsettling. We'd been dancing around whatever was between us for months now, both of us too careful, too concerned about disrupting me and Clara's friendship. His worried gaze held something deeper – a silent promise of support that made my throat tight.

Detective Lane cleared his throat. "Ms. Wilson, I know this is difficult, but I need to ask: is there anyone who might want to harm you or Benji? Any custody disputes or threats?"

I shook my head, breaking eye contact with Tom. "No, it's just been Benji and me since his father died. I don't... I can't think of anyone who'd want to hurt us."

"What about at work? Any difficult interactions recently?"

"I write articles for Style & Scenes Magazine online. All my coworkers are remote – I've never even met them in person." My voice broke. "Please, you have to find him. He's all I have."

Officer Patel placed a gentle hand on my arm. "We're mobilizing every resource we have. The Amber Alert will go out within the hour, and we already have officers retracing your route and interviewing witnesses at the mall."

Tom stepped fully into the room then, his presence solid and reassuring. "I can help coordinate with the local contractors," he said to Detective Lane. "I know every construction site within fifty miles through my work. If anyone's seen anything suspicious..."

The reality of it all crashed over me – my son's face would soon be on every news channel and highway sign. My sweet, brave little boy was out there somewhere, probably scared and confused, while I lay here helpless, unable to find him.

Chapter 3

My son was taken from me.

That was my resounding thought during the entirely unhelpful conversation with the police.

"Ms. Wilson, just a few more questions," Detective Lane said, tapping his pen against his notepad. He at least appeared intrigued by my responses, despite the fact that he couldn't get it through his thick skull that I had no idea who had done this.

Tom shifted in his chair by the window, his jaw clenched. He hadn't said a word since the questioning began, but I could feel his tension radiating across the room.

"Fine." I sighed, closing my eyes in preparation to continue the endless cycle of similar responses.

"You mentioned previously that you had no known enemies. Have you had any arguments recently? Like with a friend or boyfriend?"

I fought the urge to suck my teeth, taking another deep breath before responding. "No, as I said before, I don't have a boyfriend, Benji's father is deceased, and I was on my way to my godson's birthday party when this happened. No, my godson's mother and I weren't fighting."

At the mention of Benji's father, my heart sank a bit lower. That was another thing I remembered. My son had said that "Daddy" brought him ice cream, but I couldn't mention that to the detective. It wasn't possible and it would only muddy the investigation instead of helping it. Roman had been dead for nearly three years now.

But what if it did mean something? This was so confusing. Instead of overthinking it, I blurted my next words. "I think the ice cream man gave Benji a free cone before it happened."

Detective Lane's expression grew more serious. "The ice cream man?" He flipped open his notepad. "Describe him to me, please."

I rattled off a description – Caucasian male, late twenties, wearing a red and white striped apron and a Markie's Ice Cream cap. The more I described him, the more obvious it became to me that he had to have taken Benji.

Then I grew confused again – how could he have taken Benji if he was working the stand? I didn't see anyone else with him... Another thought came – maybe he didn't take Benji, but what if Benji went back into the mall? What if he was still there? The mall didn't close until 10PM. My son could still be there.

"Have they checked the mall?" I asked.

Detective Lane nodded. "Yes, that was one of the first things we did. The security officers contacted all the store owners and an announcement was read over the intercom. Mall security officers have searched and no one has found him yet. No one has stepped forward saying they've seen him yet either."

My heart sank further.

Detective Lane continued. "But now that you've mentioned the ice cream man, I'll have him questioned."

His tone and expression were neutral, but I sensed something behind his eyes. Contempt? Did he blame me for not making this connection sooner?

How could I, when I... Maybe I should have made the connection sooner. What was wrong with me?

Exhaustion was sweeping through me. My vision blurred as I thought of how we just celebrated Benji's seventh birthday, and now this happened. Was that the last birthday I would get to spend with my baby?

I wasn't an idiot. I knew all too well that these types of stories barely ever had a happy ending, and this was especially true the more time passed between the kidnapping and when the child was found. If ever.

Three hours. My son had been gone for three hours and he seemed to have vanished without a trace.

I didn't want to have these thoughts.

I didn't want to be in this situation.

Simultaneously, I knew there was no way out.

If I wanted to find my son, I had to cooperate with the police and we had to move fast.

The only problem was I had no idea who would do this. Everything in my life was going great. I wasn't lying when I said I had no enemies and no recent arguments. In fact, I had just been musing about the fact that for the first time in a long time, I was at peace.

And now it was all stripped away from me.

My mind couldn't help but travel once again to Roman, my high school sweetheart and Benji's father. We'd been on and off for years, fighting about everything and nothing. During one of our breaks, I met Gino. He seemed perfect at first - until the control started, then the abuse. Roman had been the one to help me escape, to convince me to press charges. And Gino... Gino had taken him from me, from our son, in a spray of bullets outside my old apartment.

I had successfully pushed the painful memories to the crevices of my mind, but now they were fighting to take over. Not today, I willed myself. Not now.

"Ms. Wilson?" Detective Lane said.

I blinked out of my thoughts. "Yes?"

At that moment, Clara, Angelique, and Peter returned to the room, with Peter chomping on a bag of potato chips. My heart sank when I saw my godson. If I had been more careful, we wouldn't be here, and Benji would be right here with Peter.

Detective Lane opened his mouth, then pressed his thin lips together. "I think these are all the questions we have for now. The Amber Alert will go out immediately and we will begin the search." He extended a card in my direction. "My contact info is on here. Feel free to call me anytime, and if you're not able to reach me, contact the station and someone will get a hold of me."

Clara reached over and took the card when my hands shook too much to grasp it. Detective Lane left the room, and Angelique squeezed my shoulder.

"We'll do everything we can to find him," she said softly.

I couldn't muster a response. This was not really happening. How could someone take my son? I followed every precaution. I went with him everywhere he went. Especially after Roman was murdered.

Chills ran down my spine at another possibility. It couldn't have been... No, he was locked up.

But what if it was someone connected to him?

"Nadine?" Clara studied me.

"Do you think Gino could have sent someone?" I blurted.

Tom straightened immediately, his eyes sharp. "Gino? That bastard's still in prison, isn't he?"

"Yes, but..." My voice trembled. "What if he arranged something? What if—"

"Call the detective back!" Clara interrupted.

"Huh?"

"Call him! Catch him before he leaves!"

Tom was already striding toward the door, his long legs eating up the distance. "Detective Lane!" his voice boomed down the hallway. "We need you back here. Now."

Chapter 4

Detective Lane was clearly irritated. "Why didn't you tell me about the murder before?"

My head throbbed viciously, making it hard to concentrate. "I... It's not something I like to think about."

He took a condescending tone with his next comment. "Let's start from the beginning, and please tell me everything. We need all bases covered if we want a chance to find your son."

I studied him, and it looked like he wanted to add, *"We still need to question the ice cream man you just mentioned,"* but he didn't.

Tom, who had refused to leave the room despite Detective Lane's attempts to dismiss him, stepped closer to my bed. His presence was oddly steadying as another wave of dizziness hit me.

My throat was dry. I reached for the cup of water Martha had left on the tray next to my bed, my hand trembling so badly that Tom had to help me steady it. Swallowing a few sips, I grimaced at the thought of this conversation.

"Three years ago, Roman was murdered by Gino, my ex-boyfriend."

Detective Lane's piercing eyes studied mine. "And is Gino Benji's father?"

I shook my head, immediately regretting the movement as pain shot through my skull. "No, Roman is his... was his father. He and I were together first, but we broke up..." My voice cracked. I couldn't do this, but I had to.

"Did you break up with him to pursue Gino?"

"No!" The word shot out of my mouth with disgust. I caught Tom's fist clenching at his side. I calmed myself, trying to focus through the fog in my brain. "No, Roman and I fought a lot, which was why we broke up. I met Gino after we ended our relationship. Gino was abusive..."

"Did he abuse Benji?"

Something about Detective Lane's tone was bothering me. It was as if he wanted to get this conversation over with, like it should have been easy for me to talk about the murder of the man I loved.

Roman and I were made for each other. We had our ups and downs like any other couple, but once we had time apart, we realized life wasn't the same.

All his attempted relationships failed, and so did mine.

Only my failed relationship took a much darker turn.

"Ms. Wilson?" Detective Lane's sharp tone cut into my thoughts.

The room swam before my eyes. I forced myself to stay on track. "No, he didn't abuse Benji, but he also didn't seem to have much interest in him. He pretended to when we first got together, but after he moved in..."

Memories swarmed me once again as I recalled exactly how Gino felt about my son.

Gino's favorite nickname for Benji was *no-count bastard*. I cringed, focusing once again on Detective Lane. "He never abused Benji. Not physically, at least."

"Has Gino contacted you recently?"

I shook my head slowly, mindful of the pain. "He can't. He's blocked from calling or writing to me, and I can't contact him either. But he may have sent someone to do this. Only I don't know why or how."

"Where were you living when this happened?"

"I was in the middle of moving from the apartment Gino and I shared. He was supposed to move out after the court case for his abuse, but instead..." My voice broke. Tom moved closer, his hand hovering near mine. "Instead, he showed up at my old apartment on the day I was set to move and shot Roman. Three times."

Detective Lane stood abruptly. "I will set up an interview with Gino and get the wheels turning in that direction. In the meantime, if you remember anything else, reach out to me."

Before I had a chance to respond, he was walking out the door.

"What a fucking—" Tom started, but cut himself off as Angelique cut in.

"What a jerk!" she said. "Why was he talking to you like that?"

I tried to shake my head but stopped at the stabbing pain. "I don't know. I guess I should have told him about Gino earlier."

Clara spoke next. "That still doesn't give him the right to treat you like crap. Is there another detective who can take over? Doesn't he have a partner or something?"

That thought dawned on me the moment she said it and I felt like a complete failure. Why was my mind not computing basic things? Did that blow to the back of my head disrupt my sense of logic?

"I don't know!" I wailed, wanting my baby back so this whole situation would be over with. "I feel like I don't know anything anymore."

"You have a concussion," Tom reminded me gently. "Don't be so hard on yourself."

But I needed to shake myself out of it. Time was running out to find my son.

Chapter 5

Despite my adamant protests, the doctors refused to discharge me until they monitored my symptoms overnight. I kept telling them I didn't give a damn about my symptoms – all I cared about was finding my son – but my words fell on deaf ears.

They came into my room every hour, checking my vitals, my vision, and ensuring my nausea and dizziness were starting to die down. Clara had to bring Peter home around midnight, but Tom and Angelique stayed overnight with me.

Officer Rachel also stayed with me, asking me questions to try to jog my nonexistent memories of what happened when Benji was taken. It was confirmed that he was indeed kidnapped after hours of searching the mall yielded no results. Detective Lane updated me about the ice cream man – apparently, he hadn't taken Benji, and he said he hadn't given Benji the ice cream for free either. According to his statement, Benji approached the stand on his own with money in hand. I didn't believe that because I hadn't given Benji any money. Detective Lane said he would question other store and stand owners nearby to find out if anyone had seen someone give Benji the money.

"He said his daddy bought him ice cream," I finally confessed, "but that's impossible because as I told you, Roman is dead."

Detective Lane seemed to consider my words. "Any other friends or relatives who might have given your son the money? Or perhaps he bought the ice cream out of his allowance?"

This was exhausting. My eyes blurred. "Benji doesn't have an allowance. The only money he had was the three quarters I gave him for the ride, and I watched him put those quarters into the slot to get on it before I went inside the clothing store."

Detective Lane seemed to accept that answer, though it still led us nowhere.

This was the worst nightmare of my life.

The next morning, I was finally discharged and allowed to go home, but I didn't want to go home. I wanted to go wherever Benji was.

Tom, Angelique, and Officer Rachel were going to accompany me to my house, but I urged Tom and Angelique to go home instead and get some rest.

"No way I'm leaving you," Tom said, and Angelique echoed his sentiments.

Now that morning had come, Clara said she was coming over too. My minivan was still at the mall, and ironically, my keys had been recovered by the same passerby who found me, so I had them in my possession, along with my purse since the officers had apparently found whatever evidence they needed from it.

My mind went frantic for a moment, and I called Detective Lane's phone, demanding that he question the passerby who said they found me in the lot but didn't see my son, but he assured me that the elderly woman had already been questioned and there was no evidence found that she had taken my son. She also didn't own the mysterious dark van that was shown on the camera footage. We were back to square one and running out of known options for who could have taken him. Which meant that the search had taken a darker turn. If a friend or relative would have taken Benji, we could at least assume he was safe. But if a stranger took him...

Tom drove me to my car, then followed me to my house where Angelique and Officer Rachel were waiting.

Once inside, they begged me to get some sleep.

"Are y'all crazy?" I yelled, though I was exhausted. I had stayed up all night in the hospital with no problem because the doctors were in and out of my room every hour, but they had given me orders to get some rest when I got home. I had zero intentions on following those orders.

"You need your rest," Officer Rachel said. "Getting some sleep might help jog your memories of what happened yesterday."

When she said those words, I was torn and heartbroken all over again. Torn because the last thing I wanted to do was sleep when my son was out there with some random stranger who could be doing all sorts of things to him, but also because I knew she was right. If I didn't get sleep, my mind would crash soon anyway. I only had a shred of sanity left as it was, and if I didn't get sleep soon, I would lose that too. I reluctantly obeyed and went to my bedroom.

When I emerged three hours later, Officer Rachel was the first to speak. She was sitting on the couch in silence but scrambled up from her seat. Tom was on his phone next to Officer Rachel scrolling, while Angelique was snoring on the loveseat.

"Nadine, that wasn't enough time," she urged. "You need more rest."

I refused to back down. "I've slept long enough. Plus, I will never be able to truly rest with my son out there."

She stared at me for a long moment before finally giving in. "Okay," she said.

"Were there any updates while I was in my room?" I asked. The first thing I had done when I woke up was check my phone for calls or texts from Detective Lane, but I saw nothing.

Officer Rachel shook her head. "No, nothing," she said, and my heart sank.

Tom looked up at me from the couch. "Don't worry, Nadine. We'll find him."

"How can we, when nobody's doing anything!"

Officer Rachel cut back in. "I can assure you, Nadine, we're doing everything we can."

My reply was sarcastic and instant. "Well, it seems like what you're doing is a whole lot of nothing if my son still hasn't been found."

My words were harsh and I knew it, but I couldn't help it. No one seemed to understand what I was going through. How could someone do this to me? What had I ever done to deserve this?

I had half a mind to snatch up my keys and go looking for Benji myself, but I knew it would be no use. If the trained police officers couldn't find him, where would I look? The mall? The building had emptied when it closed and no one had seen Benji.

He wasn't there.

He didn't seem to be anywhere.

Forcing myself to remain calm, I sat between Officer Rachel and Tom on the couch. Tom put his arm around me.

"So what do we do, just sit here and wait?" I asked.

Officer Rachel studied me. "We'll get updates from Detective Lane as the search progresses and if things escalate, we may need to do a press conference."

My heart dropped. "A press conference?" I repeated.

She nodded. "Sometimes a wider reach will help in cases like this."

I didn't like the fact that she was calling my son's abduction a case, but I let it go. The woman was only doing her job and she had stayed with me all night. I needed to back off.

Clara and Peter arrived, and Angelique woke up. Now, we were all sitting in my small but cozy living room staring at each other. My eyes kept drifting to the photos above the TV - seven years of Benji's life displayed chronologically, from his first day in the hospital to his most recent school picture. The African figurines in the glass cabinet, collected during happier times, seemed to mock me with their dancing poses. Benji's artwork, framed and hung with pride, made my heart ache. The large snake plant in the corner was one he'd helped me repot just last weekend.

Peter sat on the floor near his mother's feet, occasionally whispering questions that shattered my heart. "When is Benji coming home, Mommy?"

Clara caught my eye before pulling him close. "Soon, baby. Benji will be home soon."

Officer Rachel shifted on the couch beside me. She'd been taking notes steadily since her arrival, her calm demeanor a stark contrast to my internal chaos.

Clara had sent Tom out for pizza, despite his obvious reluctance to leave. "I'll be back in fifteen minutes, tops," he'd promised, his jaw set with worry.

Though I'd done nothing to cause this, I couldn't stop feeling like it was my fault. Who took my son? And why?

If I hadn't been so busy focusing on other things, maybe this never would have happened. My mind was on work and hurrying to get to Peter's party. Maybe if I'd been more alert, paid more attention to my surroundings, I would have seen the person coming...

My eyes widened as a fragmented memory came back to me.

There was a quick movement from my right peripheral before I was struck. I had been staring at my trunk when it happened. Along with the brief peripheral view, I caught a glimpse through the rear window of someone approaching. Was that a red jacket they were wearing? Or was my mind playing tricks on me, fabricating details that weren't there?

"Come on," I muttered under my breath as Officer Rachel stared at me.

"Nadine, are you okay?" she reached out and touched my shoulder but I jerked away.

"No, let me..." I shook my head as the memory faded. Slumping back in my seat in defeat, I felt like a failure.

"What's wrong?" Clara asked, her expression tense. Peter looked up from his spot on the floor.

Angelique was staring too. "What is it, Nadine?"

My eyes blurred. "I was trying to remember something!"

Officer Rachel remained calm despite my frustration. "What were you trying to remember?"

She spoke in a gentle soothing tone, but it only frustrated me further.

"I just... I thought I caught a glimpse of the person before they hit me. There might have been a red jacket, but..." I pressed my palms against my eyes. "I can't be sure if that's real or if my brain is making it up."

Officer Rachel leaned forward, pen poised. "Even if you're not sure, it's worth noting. Sometimes our subconscious remembers details we can't quite access yet. Was it a man or woman?" she coaxed.

I shook my head. "I can't remember. I thought I would be able to if I focused hard enough, but it's not coming back to me."

Officer Rachel inhaled a quick breath, then gave me a reassuring look. "Just give it time."

"We don't have time though," I said bluntly. "The first twenty-four hours are most crucial, remember? We've already blown past most of it since the doctors refused to discharge me last night then I spent those three hours sleeping this morning." I stood from my seat, growing antsy all over again. "We're not doing enough! I've seen how these things go. Why aren't we doing more to find my son?"

Silence filled the room as my mind traveled back to Rebekah Florence, a six-year-old girl who was abducted from our city six months ago. She was taken from her mother too, and her body was found in the woods three months later.

As if hearing my thoughts, Peter whispered in Clara's ear. "Mommy... is Benji alive?"

Clara quickly shushed him, but the damage was done. Anguish consumed me. "My baby!" I wailed.

Clara and Angelique moved closer to hold me while Officer Rachel moved to a different seat, her face etched with sympathy.

"Want me to turn on the news?" Angelique asked, and I wanted to say no, but at the same time, my brain was still malfunctioning. I said yes.

Of course, the channel was displaying the news, and Benji's smiling photo showed on the screen.

"Breaking news right outside of Briarwood Mall," the reporter said. *"We've been following this story since yesterday. An Amber Alert has been issued for seven-year-old Benjamin Wilson, who was abducted yesterday afternoon by an unknown assailant. Camera footage showed the following van near the time of the scene. If anyone has information regarding this case, please reach out to..."*

My brain tuned out the rest of her words. This was really happening. I was staring at my baby on a TV screen instead of having him right here next to me.

A knock at the door made my heart leap. Detective Lane with news? But when Rachel opened it, it was just Tom with the pizza, his face drawn with concern as he took in my tear-stained face.

How would I function without my son?

"Nadine, you need to eat something," Tom said, setting the pizza box on the coffee table.

The smell of cheese and pepperoni - Benji's favorite - turned my stomach. My boy should be here, begging for a second slice even though I always insisted he finish his first one completely.

Peter perked up at the sight of food, then immediately deflated. "I don't want any," he mumbled, pressing closer to Clara.

"Just a small piece, honey," Clara coaxed, but Peter shook his head.

"It's not fair to have pizza when Benji can't have any."

Fresh tears spilled down my cheeks. Officer Rachel handed me another tissue from the box that had been steadily emptying since I came home this morning.

"The detective will call as soon as they have anything," she assured me, though her words felt hollow. I'd seen enough of these stories to know that every minute that passed decreased our chances of...

No. I couldn't think like that.

Tom paced near the window, occasionally peeking through the blinds at the news vans that had started gathering outside. "Should we give them a statement?" he asked, his contractor's hands fidgeting like they needed something to build or fix.

"Detective Lane said to wait," Rachel reminded him gently. "We don't want to compromise the investigation."

I stared at the pizza box, remembering last Friday when Benji and I had our weekly movie night. We'd ordered pizza then too, and he'd fallen asleep on the couch halfway through *The Lion King*, pizza sauce still on his chin. I'd carried him to bed, treasuring how he still felt like my baby even though he insisted he was a "big boy" now.

"Mommy," Peter's voice cracked, "can I sleep over here tonight? To wait for Benji?"

Clara stroked his hair. "Not tonight, sweetheart. But we'll come back first thing tomorrow."

"But what if he comes home tonight? He'll want to tell me about where he was!"

The innocent hope in his voice made me want to scream. Instead, I pushed myself up from the couch, my legs shaky.

"I need some air," I managed to say, heading toward my small backyard patio. The same patio where Benji had helped me plant tomatoes in the spring, where we'd had water balloon fights in the summer, where just yesterday morning we'd eaten breakfast together.

Tom moved to follow me, but Angelique caught his arm. "Give her a minute," I heard her say as I stepped outside.

The evening air was cooling, but I barely felt it. Somewhere out there, my son was with strangers. Was he scared? Cold? Had they fed him dinner? Did they know he couldn't sleep without his stuffed tiger? That he was allergic to peanuts?

A police car cruised slowly past the house, its presence both reassuring and terrifying. They were looking for my boy, but they hadn't found him yet.

"Please," I whispered to whoever might be listening, "please bring him home."

Chapter 6

After a few hours, Peter grew irritable due to sitting around with nothing to do, and Clara gave me a pained look. I could tell she was torn between staying with me and bringing her son home. I nodded and forced a smile, then looked down at Peter, who was sitting with his back against the couch, pouting. I had already ruined the child's birthday party with my negligence, and now I was forcing him to sit in a room full of adults?

"You can take him home," I said in a soft voice, though I welled up as soon as I said the words.

"You sure?" she asked.

I nodded. "Go ahead." My voice cracked as I spoke, but I meant it. No use putting Peter through the torture of staying here all day when he didn't really understand what was going on. He was just a baby himself.

"I'm staying," Tom said with a determined expression, and my heart fluttered, but I didn't have the strength to respond. I just nodded.

"I'll stay too," Angelique said, but I shook my head.

"No girl, you go ahead." Angelique had a major test tomorrow morning. She was a graduate student getting her masters in Theology.

Angelique shook her head. "No, Nadine, I'm staying." She moved closer, her hand finding mine. "And don't you dare worry about my test."

I eyed her warily. "I thought you said it was a major part of your grade?"

She squeezed my hand. "Don't worry about that. I've already studied."

She was probably just saying that to make me feel better, but I didn't fight her. I didn't want to be a burden to my friends, but at the same time, I needed their support.

Clara gathered Peter's things, then hugged me tight. "I'll be back first thing tomorrow morning," she whispered. "And of course, I'll be calling throughout the day today too." Peter was clearly ready to go by the way he was tugging his mother's sleeve, but when he saw the expression on my face, he rushed over and wrapped his arms around my legs.

"Tee Tee, tell Benji I saved him some cake!"

My throat closed up completely.

After they left, the house felt emptier somehow, despite still having Tom, Angelique, and Officer Rachel with me. The ticking of the clock on the wall seemed louder, each second marking time without my son.

I sprang from the couch, desperate for movement. "Does anyone want—"

My phone buzzed on the coffee table, cutting me off mid-sentence. Detective Lane's name flashed on the screen.

I faced Tom with a deer in headlights look and he came rushing over. My hands trembled so badly that Tom had to help me hit the speaker button.

"Yes? Did you find Benji?" My voice sounded strange to my own ears, high and desperate.

Officer Rachel leaned forward in her seat, pen poised over her notepad. Angelique gripped my free hand.

"No, unfortunately we have not. But I was calling to give you an update on Gino."

I held my breath as I waited for him to continue. "Yes?"

Tom moved closer, his shoulder pressed against mine, steadying me.

"Apparently, your ex had bigger fish to fry."

I was confused for a second, but Detective Lane continued. "He was just released from the infirmary after being attacked by fellow inmates."

I gasped at the news, though Gino's wellbeing was the last thing on my mind. "So he knows nothing about Benji?"

"No, he doesn't, Nadine. I'm sorry. We also have been fielding calls from the hotline. An elderly gentleman says he was in the store with you at the mall and he saw someone in a red jacket talking to Benji, but..."

Every hair on my head stood on end when he said those words. The room tilted dangerously. "A red jacket?" I screeched, grabbing Tom's arm to steady myself. "Who was it? Was he able to give a description?"

Detective Lane seemed annoyed by my outburst. "As I was saying, Ms. Wilson, unfortunately, he couldn't tell if the person was male or female. They were wearing a hat and he only saw them from behind."

My heart sank so low I almost dropped the phone. Officer Rachel was writing furiously in her notepad, her expression intense.

Tom spoke up, his contractor's voice hard with frustration. "What about the camera footage?"

Detective Lane replied, his tone suggesting he was insulted by Tom asking such a question. "We've got some officers looking into it, but at this point, we're not sure if we'll be able to identify the individual."

Tom's jaw clenched. "That's bullshit, man! All those people at that mall, and no one else saw this person in the red jacket? There's got to be footage."

"I would appreciate it if you refrained from using profanity when you spoke to me, sir," Detective Lane replied.

Tom and I shared a look of disbelief. Angelique rolled her eyes so hard I thought they might stick.

Officer Rachel opened her mouth like she wanted to say something but closed it.

Tom spoke up again. "Listen, is there anyone else who can take this case? I don't like the way you're handling it."

I gasped and grabbed his arm to tell him to stop, but Detective Lane was already replying.

"Excuse me? Sir, we've been working on this case every minute since we found out Benji was taken. I can assure you that we're doing everything we can to bring him home."

"I saw the red jacket!" I blurted, to redirect the conversation. I should have mentioned it as soon as Detective Lane said the elderly gentleman saw it, but the conversation got sidetracked with Detective Lane and Tom's argument.

Detective Lane sounded shocked. "You did?"

I nodded, pressing my free hand to my throbbing temple. "Right before I was hit, I saw a flash of a red jacket."

"Good," he said coolly. "We will send someone to your home for a sketch of the assailant."

The hope that had briefly flared in my chest withered and died. "But... I'm afraid I won't be much help," I said, my voice barely a whisper.

"Why is that?"

"Because..." My eyes clouded with tears. The room started spinning again, and I felt Tom's arm slip around my waist to support me. "I only saw the jacket, and nothing else."

Officer Rachel set down her pen, her face etched with sympathy. Angelique moved closer, forming a protective circle around me with Tom. The weight of my uselessness crashed over me in waves, and I buried my face in my hands.

The silence on the other end of the phone was deafening. Finally, Detective Lane cleared his throat. "Well, that's... unfortunate. Still, we'll send someone over. Maybe working with a sketch artist will help jog your memory."

"When?" Tom demanded before I could respond. "Now?"

"Give me a couple of hours," Detective Lane replied. "We'll have..."

"A couple of hours?" Tom's voice rose. "There's a seven-year-old boy out there somewhere, and you're telling me a couple of hours?"

Officer Rachel stood, her notepad tucked under her arm. "I can make some calls," she offered quietly. "See if we can get someone here sooner."

I nodded gratefully as she stepped into the kitchen. The sound of her soft voice carrying through the wall was oddly comforting, like at least someone was doing something.

"Ms. Wilson," Detective Lane continued, ignoring Tom completely, "try to get some rest. We'll continue canvassing the area and monitoring all incoming tips."

"I already..." I started, but the call ended before I could respond. Tom muttered something under his breath that sounded like a curse.

Angelique moved to the kitchen and came back with a glass of water. "Drink," she ordered gently, pressing it into my hands. "You're dehydrated from crying."

I took a sip, but it did nothing for me. The house felt wrong, empty in a way it never had before. My eyes drifted to Benji's backpack, still sitting by the door where he'd dropped it after school a couple days ago. His black jacket hung on the hook above it, the one he'd outgrown but refused to give up.

"What if..." My voice cracked. "What if they're hurting him?"

"Don't," Tom said firmly, but gently. "Don't go there, Nadine."

"How can I not go there, Tom, when we don't know who has him?"

My panic levels were rising rapidly and I felt like I would lose it before the day was out. I couldn't do this.

Officer Rachel returned, her phone in hand. "I've got good news. There's a sketch artist who lives nearby. She's willing to come over now."

A spark of hope flickered in my chest, but fear quickly doused it. "But I told you, I only saw—"

"Sometimes," Rachel interrupted, sitting beside me, "our minds remember more than we think. And even if you only remember the jacket, that's something. The material, the style, any logos or patterns... it all helps."

I calmed slightly at her words, reasoning that she was the expert so I should listen to her. She had obviously done this before. I wanted to ask her, *"How many children have you successfully found after they were abducted?"* but I realized I didn't want the answer to that question. The only answer I wanted was the same one I had been asking since this nightmare started: Where was my son, and how could we get him back home?

"Come here," Angelique said, and extended her hands toward me.

I walked over and she bowed her head to begin a prayer. Officer Rachel bowed her head in respect too, and so did Tom.

When the prayer ended, I thanked my friend but I didn't feel any better.

Tom began pacing again, his footsteps heavy on the hardwood floor. "I should be out there looking."

"The police said to stay here," Angelique reminded him. "In case..."

She didn't finish the sentence. In case they call. In case they bring him home. In case they find...

A knock at the door made us all jump. Rachel checked her phone. "That was fast. Must be the sketch artist."

But when she opened the door, it wasn't the sketch artist.

Chapter 7

Detective Lane stood in my doorway, his expression unreadable. Behind him, a woman with steel-gray hair and kind eyes carried a large portfolio case.

"Ms. Wilson," he said, stepping inside without waiting for an invitation. "This is Sarah Kendrick, our forensic artist. I decided to bring her myself."

Tom's eyebrows shot up in surprise, and I caught Angelique hiding a small smile behind her hand. Maybe we'd judged the detective too harshly.

"Thank you," I managed to say, though my voice was barely above a whisper.

Sarah set up her materials on my dining room table, arranging her pencils with practiced precision. "Would you like to sit here?" she asked, pulling out a chair.

I moved to the table on shaky legs, hyper-aware of everyone's eyes on me. Tom hovered nearby while Angelique perched on the edge of the couch, watching intently. Officer Rachel positioned herself near the window, occasionally peeking through the blinds at the news vans still camped outside.

"Now," Sarah said, her voice gentle but professional, "I want you to close your eyes and take a few deep breaths. Try to put yourself back in that moment."

I did as she asked, though my heart raced at the thought of revisiting that terrible memory.

"You're at the mall," she continued. "You're walking to your car. Tell me everything you see."

"I..." My throat felt tight. "I'm carrying bags. Birthday presents for Peter. I'm worried about being late."

"Good," Sarah encouraged. "What else?"

"I'm at my car. The trunk is open. I'm putting the bags inside." My hands started to tremble. "Then... then I see movement. In the reflection of the rear window."

"Focus on that reflection," Sarah said softly. "Tell me about the jacket."

I squeezed my eyes tighter, trying to grab onto the fleeting image. "It's... it's bright red. Like a windbreaker material. Not thick like a winter coat."

The scratch of Sarah's pencil against paper was the only sound in the room.

"Any patterns? Logos?"

I started to shake my head, then stopped. "Wait..." Something was forming in my mind. "There might have been... something white? On the sleeve?"

More scratching sounds. "Like this?" Sarah asked.

I opened my eyes to look at her sketch. The jacket was taking shape on the paper, and seeing it made something click.

"No," I said, leaning forward. "The white part was bigger. More like a stripe that went from the shoulder down to the..." My voice trailed off as a wave of dizziness hit me.

"Nadine?" Tom was at my side instantly. "What is it?"

"I've seen that jacket before," I whispered, but when I tried to grasp the memory, it slipped away like water through my fingers.

"Where?" Detective Lane stepped closer. "Take your time."

I pressed my palms against my eyes, trying to force the memory to surface. "I... I don't know. I can't... it's right there, but I can't..."

"It's okay," Sarah said softly. "Let's focus on the jacket itself. You mentioned a white stripe. Can you tell me more about that?"

My hands were shaking so badly that Tom had to steady them with his own. "It went from the shoulder down, but..." I shook my head in frustration. "I can't remember if it was on both sides or just one. I can't even remember if the person was tall or short, man or woman..." My voice cracked.

"You're doing great," Officer Rachel assured me from her position near the window. "Every detail helps, no matter how small."

Sarah held up the sketch. The red jacket seemed to mock me from the paper, holding secrets I couldn't unlock. "How about the material? You mentioned it was like a windbreaker?"

"Yes," I latched onto this detail desperately. "The kind that makes that swishing sound when you move. But everything else is just... blank." Tears of frustration welled in my eyes. "I'm sorry. I'm trying, but..."

"Hey," Angelique moved to kneel beside my chair. "Don't apologize. Your brain went through trauma. It's normal for memories to be fragmented."

But I couldn't shake the feeling that I was failing Benji. Somewhere in my mind was information that could help find him, but I couldn't access it. I was back to square one, with nothing but a red jacket that could belong to anyone.

"Maybe if we take a break," Sarah suggested, setting down her pencil. "Sometimes pushing too hard can block memories rather than unlock them."

Detective Lane nodded. "We can try again in a little while. You've given us something to work with, Ms. Wilson. That's more than we had an hour ago."

But their encouragement felt hollow as I stared at the partial sketch, wondering if the person wearing that jacket was with my son right now, and why I couldn't remember more about them when it mattered most.

Chapter 8

After another half hour, the sketch artist left and I had never felt more defeated in my life. What was wrong with me? Why wasn't my memory working?

Tom noticed me getting emotional, so he put his arm around me and pulled me close. We were sitting on the couch next to each other. Angelique was fighting to keep her eyes open on the loveseat, and Officer Rachel sat on one of my kitchen chairs that had been dragged into the living room.

Everything was too silent. We should have been saying more. We should have been doing more.

An email notification popped up on my phone and my eyes widened. I swiped down on the screen, heart clenching when I saw that it was my boss, Dexter. The subject of the message read: *Did you forget about me?*

The message was short and sweet. *Nadine, we need that Lansing article, pronto.*

I didn't know how to respond to him. There was no way I'd be able to submit that article today.

I looked at Tom as if he had the answers.

"What is it?" he asked, then looked down at my phone to read the message.

I swallowed. "I don't know what to say to him."

Tom studied me. "Do you want me to write him a quick reply?"

I exhaled and nodded, a tear sliding down my cheek that I quickly swiped away.

Tom gently took the phone from my hands. "Were you able to finish the article?"

I shook my head, my voice cracking as I spoke. "I... have a draft."

Tom nodded, then his fingers flew across the screen.

Feeling incapable of doing anything more, I watched as he typed.

Dexter, I'm sorry, but I only have a draft of the article. I'm unfortunately dealing with a family emergency right now and might need a few days off. My son was abducted yesterday afternoon.

When he finished, he looked at me and I nodded.

He was about to click Send, but I stopped him. "Wait, I can send my draft." I navigated to my documents folder and attached the draft, then hit Send.

Seconds later, Dexter called me.

My heart dropped. I wasn't sure what to say to him.

Tom took over once again. "Hello?" he answered, putting Dexter on speaker phone.

"Hi..." Dexter sounded cautious, probably because he expected to hear my voice. "May I speak with Nadine, please?"

Tom glanced at me before responding. "She's unable to come to the phone right now. As you can imagine, she's distraught, sir."

Dexter's voice was full of sympathy. "I understand. Please tell her she can take all the time she needs, and we're praying for her."

"Thank you, sir."

Tom ended the call and I felt a little lighter.

Then I felt like an imbecile. Why couldn't I send the email? Why couldn't I answer the call? Why was my brain stuck?

My breathing grew labored, but Tom held me again. "Chill, Nadine. You're good. It's handled."

He said that so confidently, and he was right - my job was handled. But my baby...

After I calmed, I sat back on the couch, leaning against the soft cushion and closing my eyes, trying to relax to see if I could remember that damn jacket.

I thought back as gently as I could, until the memories of earlier that day began to resurface...

I was walking through the mall. I was yelling at Benji and throwing away his ice cream. I set off the alarm on the way out of the store. I threatened him and told him he wouldn't be able to go to Peter's party. I wasn't watching him hard enough. I wasn't aware of my surroundings. I couldn't make out the person in the red jacket. I...

"Nadine? Nadine, wake up! You're having a nightmare."

Someone was forcefully shaking me. My eyes popped open and the first thing that I noticed was sunlight streaming through the windows. Angelique's purse was gone from its spot by the door, and a blanket had been draped over me sometime during the night.

My mouth felt like cotton, and my clothes were wrinkled and twisted around my body. I could feel my hair sticking up on one side where I'd been sleeping against the couch.

"What the fuck?" I rubbed my eyes, then stared at Tom, who had dark circles under his eyes. "I fell asleep? You let me sleep?"

Tom grew tongue-tied. "Nadine... I... you needed to rest."

"Damn my rest, Tom! Where the hell is my son!"

Tom wrapped me up in his arms to stop my panic attack. "Nadine, chill. Calm down. I stayed up the whole time. Nothing happened, trust me."

I pulled back and studied him. From the tiredness of his eyes, the stubble on his chin, I could tell he was telling the truth. I swallowed, allowing myself to calm, though I felt terrible for falling asleep at such a time like this. My son was out there cold and defenseless, and I was curled up on the couch asleep?

Disgust filled my veins, but Tom forced me to look at him. "You needed to rest," he assured me, and I knew he was right, though I didn't believe him.

Just then, Officer Rachel entered the room, her uniform slightly rumpled from sitting in it all night. "Everything okay?" she asked.

I was about to ask where she just came from, but I put two and two together. She came from the direction of the bathroom.

"Yes, everything is fine," Tom replied.

But everything wasn't fine. It never would be until we found my son.

Detective Lane called my phone. I jerked to answer it, praying that the nightmare was over and he had finally found Benji, but he hit me with bad news instead.

"Ms. Wilson, unfortunately we're going to have to escalate the search. We need to set up a press conference and organize search teams so we can try to find Benji."

I felt like scum at his words. If I hadn't fallen asleep on the couch, we could have been searching for my son yesterday.

My eyes shot to Tom's, a feeling of betrayal sweeping through me, but I let it go. He had stayed up all night watching me sleep while he hadn't gotten any sleep himself. Benji was no relation to Tom, so he really didn't have to do that for me. I needed to focus. I needed to think straight.

"Okay," I said after exhaling a deep breath. "Tell me what I need to do for the press conference."

The next hour passed in a blur of activity. Clara arrived with coffees and went to my bedroom to throw together a clean outfit for me. While I changed, I could hear Tom and Officer Rachel moving furniture, making space for the news crews that would be arriving.

When I emerged from the bathroom, Detective Lane and a specialist were there to prep me for the conference.

I swallowed the lump in my throat and listened to the instructions.

I went back into the bathroom to check my appearance once more. My hair was somewhat tame, and I was wearing fresh clothes, but I didn't at all feel like me. It was as if I was just going through the motions while my mind and heart were on Benji. My living room had been transformed. News cameras were being set up, and a small podium had appeared near the fireplace. The curtains were closed so the sunlight wouldn't interfere with the camera footage, and an uneasy feeling swept over me as I considered all that was happening.

The only thing that kept resounding in my ears was that my son's case had escalated, which meant he could never be found, or worse... he could be found, but not alive. I swallowed, my eyes blurring with fresh tears.

Detective Lane approached me, his tie perfectly straight despite putting in long hours trying to find Benji. "Are you ready, Ms. Wilson?"

No, I wasn't ready. I would never be ready for this.

But I nodded anyway.

The lights from the cameras were blinding as I stepped up to the podium. My hands gripped the edges so tight my knuckles turned white. The room was packed with reporters, their phones and recorders held out like accusing fingers.

"Hello..." I said, the microphone squeaking as my trembling voice let loose. A wave of feedback made me wince. "If anyone out there has seen my son, please tell me. I need..." My eyes blurred with tears. "I need him home."

Camera shutters clicked rapidly. Reporters called out questions that blended together into white noise.

"Ms. Wilson, any updates on the dark van?"

"What about the person in the red jacket?"

"Was it a man or woman who took your son?"

These were basic questions that I should have had the answers to, but I couldn't answer any of them. I had never felt more weak and powerless in my life. Through my tears, I could see Tom standing at the back of the room, his face tight with concern.

After the press conference, everything was set into motion. The police worked to organize groups while I sat there bewildered and heartbroken. Within a few short hours, the search team gathered in my front yard. Parents from Benji's school stood in clusters, studying maps that Detective Lane's team had brought. Clara organized them into groups while Angelique handed out flyers with Benji's picture.

Tom worked with the police to coordinate the search areas. They started with the mall, marking off sections on a large map spread across the hood of a police car. Teams were assigned to nearby woods, lakes, abandoned buildings, and every surrounding area that one would think an abducted child would be.

The sun climbed higher in the sky as the searchers spread out. I watched some of the teams from my porch, feeling simultaneously grateful and helpless. Every few minutes, someone would check their phone, hoping for news.

As the day wore on, my hope deflated. The autumn air grew colder, and clouds began gathering overhead. One by one, search teams returned, shaking their heads before heading out to new areas.

Detective Lane kept calling with updates, but each time there was no news.

My heart sank further and further until his final phone call, where he announced that they would have to call the search party off for today, but they would start back up again tomorrow.

"Don't worry, Ms. Wilson," he said. "We've got all hands on deck here."

He tried to sound encouraging, but his words fell on deaf ears.

The search teams trudged back, their clothes dirty from searching through undergrowth, their faces showing the same devastation I felt. As they left, each one promised to return tomorrow, but I barely heard them.

I watched the sun set from my porch, the sky turning a deep purple that reminded me of the painful lump on the back of my head. Tom sat beside me, neither of us speaking.

I was officially losing my mind.

Chapter 9

The shadows in my living room grew longer as night settled in. The house felt different in the dark - bigger, emptier. Every creak made me jump, thinking maybe, just maybe, it was Benji coming home.

Looking at Tom slumped in his chair, dark circles under his eyes, it hit me that he hadn't slept since this nightmare began. He had been a permanent fixture by my side, but exhaustion was clearly taking its toll.

"You should go," I urged, though my chest tightened at the thought of him leaving.

Tom shook his head, stifling a yawn. "No, I'm not gonna leave you, Nadine."

Angelique, who had been quietly scrolling through her phone, looked up. "Tom, go ahead. I'll stay the night. You need your rest."

Tom looked torn, his eyes moving between me and the door. "Go," I insisted, forcing strength into my voice that I didn't feel.

He gave me a lingering look before reluctantly standing. "I'll be here first thing in the morning," he declared, his voice rough with fatigue.

"Take your time," I said. "I know you have your business to attend to."

He was shaking his head before I finished speaking. "I'm not worried about that. All I care about is getting Benji home."

The words "getting Benji home" sent a fresh wave of panic through me. I pressed my nails into my palms, trying to block out the visions that had been haunting me all day - Benji crying out for me, scared and alone somewhere I couldn't reach him.

This was the worst feeling I'd ever experienced. I would wish it on no one.

"Call me when you get home," I choked out, and Tom grimly nodded.

"I will."

My heart sank when he left, though I knew he needed rest even more than I did.

Twenty minutes later, my phone buzzed with a text from him. *I'm home, but call me if anything happens. I mean it, Nadine. I don't care how late it is.*

A smile played on my lips - the first one since this entire ordeal began and I wrote back a quick reply. *You know I will.*

I was telling the truth. Tom had treated Benji's abduction like it was his own son who was missing. I would never forget the time or care he put in.

Welling up, I sniffled then trudged to the couch to sit down.

Officer Rachel had left us with an assistant during the day for the search party - probably to go home and get sleep herself, but now she was back, looking more refreshed than I would ever feel.

Clara was here earlier too, but she had to bring Peter home so he could go to sleep.

"And then there were three," I said glumly, staring into the distance as Angelique curled up on the loveseat and Officer Rachel remained in the kitchen chair. I looked over at her.

"Do you want to sit on the couch?" I asked.

She nodded, her face reddening as she stiffly walked over and sank into the soft cushions on the opposite end from me.

Now I felt like an asshole. So consumed with my own thoughts that I hadn't shown this woman a shred of hospitality.

"Are you hungry?" I asked, but she shook her head.

"Oh no, I'm fine. I already ate earlier."

"There's still some of that pizza in the fridge if you do get hungry," I said. Then I looked at my friend. "You too, Angelique."

Angelique looked up at me from her phone. "Have you eaten anything?"

I opened my mouth, then closed it before saying, "I'm not worried about food."

"Nadine..." Angelique warned. "You need to eat something. I'm serious. I let you slide yesterday but I won't let you starve yourself."

I sat numbly as she traveled to the kitchen to warm me up some pizza. When she brought it to me, along with some red juice from the fridge, I burst into tears.

"What's wrong?" she said.

I stared at the cup. "That's Benji's juice!"

Under normal circumstances, my friend would have probably told me I was acting crazy, but she didn't this time. Instead, she quietly handed me the plate of pizza then headed to the kitchen to switch out the juice for a water bottle.

When she returned, I was staring down at the plate.

"What's wrong?"

I looked up at her with glassy eyes. "How can I eat when he is out there starving?"

Angelique sat next to me and put her arm around me. "Honey, we don't know that."

I swallowed. "That's the problem, Angelique. We don't know anything."

She fell silent for a moment, then said, "Listen if we're going to get through this, you need your strength. Eat, Nadine. Just one slice. Please."

I knew my friend was right. I needed to eat, though I didn't want to.

The pizza sat in front of me, growing cold. The smell that usually made my mouth water now turned my stomach. Each bite felt like a betrayal - how could I eat when I didn't know if my son had food?

My hands shook as I picked up the smallest slice. The cheese had congealed, and the crust felt like cardboard in my mouth. I forced myself to chew, counting each bite. *One, two, three...* thinking about Benji's little face the last time we'd had pizza together, how he always picked off the pepperoni and lined them up on his plate.

Then I forced myself to eat the rest of it before pushing the plate of the other slices onto Angelique's lap. "That's all I can take right now," I said.

She gave me an encouraging smile. "I suppose it's better than nothing."

She disappeared into the kitchen while Officer Rachel continued writing in her notebook. What was she writing over there? Was she taking notes about me? What was she saying?

Angelique returned from the kitchen. "Want me to turn on the news?" she offered.

I sighed, then nodded.

Angelique used the remote to turn on the TV and the same reporter from before was speaking about my son. They highlighted all that had happened with the search party, which ultimately amounted to nothing. After the story ran a few more times, I changed the channel.

Angelique settled into her phone, and I pretended to watch a sitcom while agonizing over my son.

About half an hour later, my eyelids were growing heavy, but I wouldn't dare sleep. Then, Angelique's voice cut through the silence.

"What the hell?" Her sharp tone startled me.

"What is it?" I demanded.

She pulled an earbud from her ear. "Nadine..." She eyed me. "I don't want you to see this, but..."

"Don't want me to see what?" My heart raced with fear. "What happened? Is it Benji?"

My eyes shot to my phone, but there were no missed calls or texts.

"What is it, Angelique?"

Officer Rachel looked intrigued too.

Angelique swallowed, then walked over and removed her earbuds from her cell phone, allowing the video she was watching to play aloud.

It was a social media commentator giving his spiel on Benji's abduction. *"It seems that everyone isn't so convinced about the authenticity of the child's mother,"* he said. *"Here is what one man had to say about Ms. Wilson."*

My jaw dropped as the camera shot to the man from the ice cream stand in the mall. *"She threw the kid's ice cream in the trash!"* he exclaimed. *"Then she gave me a dirty look and a few hours later, the police are questioning me? It was totally uncalled for, and she yanked that kid into that store too forcefully for my liking. I don't wanna speak on it too harshly, but some people aren't fit to be parents. I mean...*"

The camera shot back to the commentator. *"Yikes!"* he said with a cringe-face. *"Seems like the police might need to do some digging into that boy's momma, I'm just saying..."*

"Turn that off," Officer Rachel said in a stern tone.

Angelique and I turned to her with wide eyes.

Her expression softened. "Trust me, you don't want to go down a social media rabbit hole. People can be unbelievably cruel in times like this, but you have to ignore it, Nadine."

It was the first time she had called me by my first name.

I stared at her. "How could they say something like this?"

Officer Rachel looked as if it pained her to speak. "Unfortunately, it's par for the course. Some people use stories like this to gain a spotlight for themselves. Please, do your best to ignore it."

She was trying to encourage me, I knew it, but that man's words were seared into my brain. He basically called me an unfit mother.

And the commentator acted like he agreed with him.

These men didn't know me. How dare they?

I forced myself to calm, leaning back against the couch as Angelique went back to the loveseat.

Try as I might, I couldn't let go.

I opened my phone and navigated to social media, putting the volume on mute and searching for the video using my search bar. It immediately popped up, and my heart sank when I saw it had over three thousand views and seven hundred likes.

Seven hundred people thought I didn't deserve Benji.

My vision blurred as I scrolled through the comments. Each one felt like a physical blow.

Bad mother.

Something's not right.

Why isn't anyone investigating her?

The blue light from my phone cast a sickly glow in the dark room. Outside, a car drove past, its headlights sweeping across the wall. For a moment, I imagined it was Benji coming home, but the sound faded away, leaving only the quiet hum of the heating system and Angelique's soft breathing from the loveseat.

Officer Rachel cleared her throat. "Ms. Wilson-Nadine," she corrected herself, her voice gentler than I'd heard it before. "You should try to rest."

But how could I rest? These strangers' words echoed in my head, mixing with my own guilty thoughts about that day at the mall. And somewhere out there, my son was missing.

I had a sinking feeling that this was just the beginning - that these voices would only get louder, more accusatory. And I didn't know how much more I could take.

Chapter 10

My mind swam throughout the night, even as Angelique snored peacefully and Officer Rachel fought to keep her eyes open. She kept peeking over at me as if she was trying to see if I had fallen asleep.

After a couple of hours of this, it dawned on me that she was probably doing that in hopes that I had fallen asleep so that she could sleep.

What a dunce I'd been lately. A total failure. An unfit mother just like those people said online. Closing my eyes, I slowed my breathing so Officer Rachel would think I was asleep. It did the trick. Soon, she was snoring softly just like Angelique. A hole had formed in my heart as the weight of all that was happening began to consume me. I warily opened my eyes, listening as crickets chirped outside my windows and cars sporadically rolled by. As much as I wanted to succumb to sleep, I would not allow my body to rest. If I could not do anything else for my son, I could stay awake until he was returned to me.

The sun was barely peeking through my curtains when Detective Lane's knock jolted both Angelique and Officer Rachel awake. I was already up, of course, sitting in the same position I'd been in all night.

Bounding to the door and praying it was Benji, I whipped it open, my heart sinking when I saw that my son was not with the detective.

Detective Lane looked better rested than any of us as he settled into the chair across from me. "We've been reviewing the mall footage." He pulled out his notepad. "We got a clear shot of the person in the red jacket, but..." He hesitated.

"But what?"

"They knew what they were doing. Never turned toward the camera. Always kept their head down or angled away."

My stomach churned. "So we have nothing?"

"We have more than we did yesterday," he assured me. "We know their approximate height, build. The footage shows them following you at a distance before..."

Before they took my son. I couldn't bear to hear him say it.

"Detective," I started, then stopped, wondering if I should even mention it. "There's this video online..."

His expression told me he already knew. "The ice cream vendor. Yes, we're aware."

"They're saying I..." My voice cracked.

"Ms. Wilson, listen to me carefully." He leaned forward. "In cases like this, people come out of the woodwork. They want their fifteen minutes of fame, they want to feel important. We can't control what they say, but we can't let it distract us from finding Benji."

My phone buzzed. A text from Clara: *You need to see this. Call me.*

I stepped into the kitchen to call her, my hands shaking as I dialed.

"Have you seen it?" she asked without saying hello.

"Seen what?"

"I'm sending it now. Some woman who claims she saw you that day..."

The video loaded, showing a middle-aged woman with perfectly styled hair sitting in what looked like an expensive car. *"I saw that mother,"* she was saying, her voice dripping with judgment. *"She was acting so suspicious in that store. Setting off alarms, rushing out... I mean, who knows what she was really doing in there? And the way she treated that poor child..."*

The comments were worse than the video:

Bet she staged the whole thing to cover up the shoplifting!

Someone check her record!

What kind of mother...

Before I could stop myself, I was typing: *You don't know anything about me or my son. You weren't there. You don't know what happened!*

The responses came flooding in:

Oh, look who showed up instead of looking for her kid.

Someone found her mugshot from 2019!

No wonder the kid's gone.

My fingers flew across the keypad to further defend myself, to tell them that there was no way they had found a mugshot on me because I had never been arrested a day in my life, but that was before I saw a new comment that popped up.

Someone had made a meme of my tear-stained face from the press conference, with text that read: *When shoplifting goes wrong...* It already had hundreds of shares.

I dropped my phone like it had burned me, but Detective Lane was already beside me, picking it up.

"This stops now," he said firmly, closing the social media apps. "These people? They don't matter. What matters is finding Benji. That's it. Everything else is noise."

But it wasn't noise. It was my life being torn apart in public while my son was still missing. And there wasn't a damn thing I could do about either.

Chapter 11

The search party was gathering at 10 AM at the community center. As Tom drove us there, I kept checking my phone, rereading those horrible comments. That was when I saw it - a new post from the ice cream vendor, updating his "story" with even more accusations.

"Can we stop at the mall?" I asked suddenly. "It's on the way, and I... I just need to check something before the search starts."

Tom hesitated. "Nadine, we should get to the community center. There are already fifty people waiting..."

"Please. Five minutes. I keep thinking that if I go stand near the store where I was shopping, I'll be able to recreate the imagery from that day. Maybe I saw the person wearing the red jacket in the mall but didn't realize it." The lie felt bitter in my mouth, but I couldn't help myself.

Officer Rachel, who was riding with us to the search, sighed. "Five minutes. The mall's security office is already cooperating with the investigation, but if it will help you focus on the search..."

I tuned her out and nodded, waiting on pins and needles as we traveled to the mall. We couldn't get there quickly enough.

When we arrived, Officer Rachel tried to warn me again. "Remember Nadine, we don't have time..."

I barely processed the rest of her sentence as I hurried into the huge building. The mall was filling up with morning shoppers. And there the bastard was, setting up his ice cream stand, just like every other morning - as if he hadn't helped destroy what was left of my life.

I stalked up to him before anyone could stop me.

"Nadine!" Tom called after me.

The vendor looked up as I approached, recognition dawning on his face.

"You," I said, my voice shaking. "How dare you?"

"Ma'am, I-"

"My son is missing," I choked out, aware of people starting to stare. "My son is out there somewhere, and you're online telling lies about me?"

Tom caught up to me, grabbing my arm. "Nadine, don't. Think about the search party. Think about finding Benji."

"You don't know me!" I was shouting now, tears streaming down my face. "You don't know anything about me or my son! How could you..."

Officer Rachel appeared on my other side as mall security approached. The ice cream vendor backed away, hands raised.

"He's seven years old," I sobbed as Tom and Officer Rachel tried to guide me away. "He's just a baby, and instead of helping find him, you..."

"Come on Nadine," Tom said. "We need to..."

"Wait!" I called out, wrenching myself from their arms and approaching the ice cream man again. He was holding out his cell phone, probably recording me Live, but I didn't care. My question was more important than his search for clout.

I swiped his phone and it clattered to the floor.

"Hey!" He yelled at me but I was already asking my question.

"Who bought my son that ice cream?"

"What?" He asked like he was confused while trying to reassemble his phone. The battery had fallen out when it fell on the floor.

I rephrased my question. "You said my son came to your stand with money in hand, but that's not true. I didn't give my son any money. Who bought him the ice cream?"

He stared at me but didn't put his phone back in my face.

"Look lady, I have no idea. I wasn't watching your son – that was your job."

His words were said in a biting tone but I ignored the feeling they gave me as he continued.

Once he saw how desperately I was listening for his answer, he softened up.

His voice lowered in octave. "Look, I already told the police that I didn't see anybody else near the kid. He bought the cone, and the next thing I knew, you were screaming at him and throwing it in the trash."

"I didn't..." I protested, but he held up his hands.

"That's all I saw, okay?"

We stared at each other.

"I have to get back to work." He gestured with his thumb toward his stand.

Tears slipped down my cheeks as I nodded and I retreated, following Tom and Officer Rachel out of the mall.

Back in the car, Officer Rachel made a call while Tom tried to calm me down. "The search party," I suddenly remembered, horrified. "All those people are waiting..."

"Detective Lane will start them off," Officer Rachel said, covering her phone. "We'll meet them at the second checkpoint. But Nadine..." She turned to face me. "You need to focus. Channel this energy into finding Benji. These other people? They don't matter."

But as we drove to meet the search party, all I could think about was how I'd just given that man more ammunition. I could already imagine his next post: *Unstable mother attacks innocent vendor...*

I had to pull myself together. For Benji.

"I'm sorry," I whispered. "I just... when I saw him standing there like nothing had happened..."

"We understand," Tom said softly, but I could hear the worry in his voice.

When we arrived at the search area, I could see groups of people already spreading out through the woods near the mall. Detective Lane broke away from the main group and headed toward our car.

"There you are," he said, then paused, taking in my tear-stained face. "Everything okay?"

"I made a mistake," I admitted. "At the mall, I-"

"Already heard," he cut me off, not unkindly. "Listen, Nadine. I know you're going through hell right now. But we need you clear-headed. These volunteers?" He gestured to the scattered groups of searchers. "They're here for Benji. Not because of some ice cream vendor's video, not because of social media. They're here because a little boy is missing, and they want to help find him."

I nodded, wiping my eyes. He was right. I couldn't fall apart now.

"We've divided the area into grids," Detective Lane continued. "Your group will take section E, just past that ridge. Officer Rachel will stay with you. Tom, I need you with Group C - they're short a team leader."

As we gathered our supplies - water bottles, whistles, bright orange vests - my phone buzzed again. I didn't need to look to know what it was. More comments. More accusations. More people who thought they knew the truth.

I switched off my phone and shoved it deep into my pocket. Let them talk. Let them speculate. I had a job to do.

"I'm coming, baby," I whispered as we headed toward our search area. "Mommy's going to find you."

But even as I forced myself to focus on the search, a small voice in my head wondered if I'd just made things worse. If my outburst would somehow hurt our chances of finding Benji. If I was proving all those cruel commenters right.

No. I couldn't think like that. My son needed me strong, focused, determined. Everything else was just noise.

The day wore on. Every few minutes, someone would shout "Over here!" and my heart would stop, only to restart painfully when it turned out to be nothing - a discarded toy that wasn't Benji's, a piece of clothing that was too old, a broken branch that meant nothing at all.

The sun beat down mercilessly. Officer Rachel kept trying to make me drink water, but my throat felt too tight to swallow. We combed through section E methodically, looking behind every tree, under every bush. I kept seeing flashes of blue - Benji's favorite color - but it was always just a wrapper, a plastic bag, a bird.

"Benji!" My voice was getting hoarse from calling. Other voices echoed through the woods, some familiar, some strange, all calling my son's name. "Benji, baby, are you here?"

Around six o'clock, Detective Lane called for a brief rest. I didn't want to stop, but my legs were shaking from exhaustion.

"We've covered almost eight miles," he announced to the gathered groups. "We'll take thirty minutes, then start on the expanded perimeter."

Tom brought me a sandwich I couldn't eat. "You need to keep your strength up," he insisted.

I watched the volunteers during the break - teachers from Benji's school, parents I recognized from football practice, complete strangers who'd seen the news. They looked tired but determined. A woman I'd never met was showing everyone a map on her tablet, suggesting places to check next.

"Time to move out," Detective Lane called.

We searched until the light began to fade. Every step that didn't lead to Benji felt like a failure. Every empty clearing was another blow to my hope.

Finally, as darkness crept in, Detective Lane gathered everyone together. I knew what he was going to say before he opened his mouth, but I still wasn't ready to hear it.

"We're losing daylight," he announced. "We'll resume first thing tomorrow morning, starting with the north sector."

"No," I said, my voice breaking. "Please, we can't stop. He's out here somewhere. He's waiting for us to find him."

The detective placed a gentle hand on my shoulder. "Nadine, we have teams with infrared equipment taking over for the night shift. But these volunteers need rest, and so do you."

"I can't go home. Not without him. Not again." The tears I'd been holding back all day finally spilled over.

People were packing up around us, their flashlight beams dancing through the trees. Some stopped to hug me, to promise they'd be back tomorrow, to tell me not to lose hope. But with each passing hour, that hope felt more and more like a cruel joke.

Tom had to practically carry me to the car. As we drove away, I pressed my face against the window, straining to see into the darkening woods. Was Benji out there, scared and alone? Was he somewhere else entirely? Was he...

No. I couldn't finish that thought.

"We'll find him," Officer Rachel said from the back seat, but her voice lacked the conviction it had held yesterday.

The house was dark when we pulled up. I'd left lights on this morning, but Angelique must have come by and turned them off. It looked empty. Lifeless.

Like a home without its child.

"I can stay," Tom offered. "Or we could call Angelique..."

I shook my head. I needed to be alone with my failure. Another day gone, another night without my son.

Despite my protests about company, Officer Rachel was required to stay with me, and Tom refused to back down. Angelique had to submit an assignment, but she said she would be back in the morning.

Inside my desolate home, I sank onto Benji's bed, clutching his favorite stuffed dinosaur. "I'm sorry," I whispered into the quiet room. "I'm so sorry, baby. Where are you? Please... please just come home."

But only silence answered, and somewhere in that silence, I felt the last pieces of my hope beginning to crack.

Chapter 12

Three weeks later...

I had nothing left to give.

Almost a month's worth of agonizing days and my baby still wasn't home. As each day passed, the number of volunteers for search parties dwindled, until they stopped altogether. I was back to my core group of Tom, Clara, and Angelique.

Benji's bedroom door stayed closed now. I couldn't bear to see his unmade bed, his dinosaur collection gathering dust. Sometimes I thought I heard his laugh echoing down the hallway, only to remember it was just another cruel trick of my mind. The house felt wrong - too quiet, too empty, too dead.

Officer Rachel was no longer staying at my house, though she called me every day with updates. Detective Lane's calls used to be multiple times a day, but now he had trickled down to once every few days. Yesterday, when he called, I could hear the shift in his voice. That subtle change in tone that meant he was starting to see Benji as a case file rather than a missing little boy.

The community center's bulletin board, once crowded with search party sign-up sheets and maps, now held only a single flyer with Benji's picture. Someone had written "Still Missing" across the top in fresh marker - probably Clara, trying to keep people from forgetting.

The sight of it made my stomach turn. *Still missing.* Like it was just a status update, not my entire world falling apart.

I barely recognized myself in the mirror anymore. Dark circles had become permanent features under my eyes, and my clothes hung loose - when was the last time I'd actually eaten a full meal? Tom kept bringing food, but everything tasted like ash. Angelique had started marking dates on my kitchen calendar when I managed to eat something substantial, like I was a patient they were monitoring.

The social media uproar had died down, except for one random asshole who kept contacting me from different accounts. *Little bitch, you better hope I find him first...* was the first message he sent. I immediately forwarded it to Detective Lane and Officer Rachel. They tried to track it but it was from a burner profile.

The second message came from a different number. *Think this is a fucking game? Like I don't know what you did? Wait til I catch up with you.*

Each new message sent my heart racing, not from fear for myself, but from the terrible hope that this person might actually know something about Benji. What if they really did know where he was? What if ignoring them meant missing a chance to find him?

Once I received that second message, Tom all but moved into my house. He started sleeping on my couch, despite my protests. Detective Lane tried to trace the number, but once again, he couldn't.

"Could he be the person who took Benji?" I asked, hating the desperate edge in my voice.

Detective Lane pursed his lips. "It's a possibility, but our analysis team is leaning toward no. This is likely someone who is set on antagonizing you to get under your skin."

I had no idea who would do such a thing. Detective Lane's encouragement didn't make me feel much better. But since the person kept texting me from different numbers, I was powerless to stop them.

Die bitch, DIE! was the message I received this morning.

It had become a routine: toss and turn throughout the night, wake up, show Tom my latest text message, have him hurl a few expletives about the bastard who was sending them, and pine over my son. Rinse and repeat.

Last night, I found myself sitting in Benji's closet at 3 AM, breathing in the fading scent of him from his favorite Batman hoodie. The fabric was still soft against my cheek, but it didn't smell like him anymore. Soon, even that would be gone.

"I know you're out there," I whispered into the darkness. "I know you're waiting for Mommy to find you. I won't stop looking, baby. I promise."

But as I sat there, surrounded by his clothes and toys, another voice - one I didn't want to acknowledge - whispered back: *What if there's nothing left to find?*

Chapter 13

The call came at midnight. I almost didn't answer the unknown number, but after several weeks of Benji being gone, I answered every call.

"Hello?" I rubbed my eyes, trying to adjust to the darkness.

"You stupid whore!"

I shot up in bed, bewildered by the harsh tone. The voice was familiar but distorted with rage. "Are you happy now? Are you fucking happy?"

I pressed speaker phone and raced into the living room to wake Tom, who was already scrambling up from the couch, reaching for his phone to record.

"Who is this?" I asked.

"Don't play dumb with me, you little slut. My son is dying because of you!"

The accent. The fury. Suddenly I knew. "Benita?"

"Yes, you dirty bitch! Gino is on life support and it's all your fault!"

My mind reeled. Benita, my ex Gino's mother. All this time, the threatening messages had been coming from Gino's mother? It couldn't be. I had to be sure though.

I looked at Tom, and he gestured for me to keep talking, angling his phone screen toward me to show that he was recording.

"Have you been texting me from all those different numbers?"

"Yes, I did, bitch! It was me. Are you happy now that my son is dying?"

My mind was reeling as I struggled to catch up with the news. "How is this my fault, Benita? I haven't seen Gino since..."

Benita didn't let me finish. "Since that detective came asking questions about your bastard child! Now my son gets into fights and they almost killed him..." Her voice broke into a blundering mess before she resumed an even tone. "They say he might not make it through the night!"

Tom moved closer to me, his hand on my shoulder. I was shaking.

"I don't understand," I said. "What does Gino getting into prison fights have to do with me?"

"Everything! Everything is because of you!" Benita's voice rose to a shriek. "If you hadn't spread your legs for that boy, Gino would still be free! He would be home with me, not dying in some prison hospital!"

The room seemed to tilt sideways. "Are you serious right now? Gino is in prison because he murdered Roman. He murdered the love of my life in cold blood!"

"Because you made him do it! You broke his heart! That boy meant nothing - nothing! But you destroyed my son's life for him!"

Tom tried to take the phone. "Ms. Benita, this is Tom. Nothing that's happening to Gino is Nadine's fault..."

"Shut the fuck up, nigga! You don't know anything! None of you know what you did to my family!" She was sobbing now, but the rage hadn't left her voice. "First you take my son's freedom, now you take his life. And for what? For that dead boy? For your bastard child?"

My blood ran cold. "What do you know about Benji?"

"I know you better not leave your house if you know what's good for you. You think you know pain? You ain't seen nothing yet."

The line went dead.

I stared at the phone, my hands trembling so hard I nearly dropped it. "It was her. All this time, it was Gino's mother sending those messages."

Tom was already dialing. "I'm calling Detective Lane right now."

"I never... we never got along, but this?" I pressed my hands against my temples, trying to make sense of it.

"Detective Lane?" Tom put his phone on speaker. "We just got a call from Gino's mother Benita. She's been the one sending the threatening messages..."

As Tom relayed the conversation, I sank onto the couch. Could she have taken Benji? Was this her twisted idea of revenge?

"We'll look into it," Detective Lane said. "I'll send a car to park outside your house tonight, Nadine. And I'll check on Gino's status at the prison hospital."

After we hung up, Tom sat beside me. "We'll figure this out."

But I barely heard him. All I could think about was Benita's words: *You think you know pain? You ain't seen nothing yet.*

What if she had my baby? What if all this time, while we were searching woods and abandoned buildings, Benji was with his father's murderer's mother?

The thought made me sick.

Chapter 14

Detective Lane's call came just after dawn. "Gino passed away at 3:42 this morning."

I sat with that information, feeling nothing but a hollow ache. Another death. More pain. When would it end?

An hour later, Angelique stopped by before her morning classes. "I brought coffee," she said, but before she could set the cups down, we heard tires screeching, then a car door slamming outside, then the screaming that quickly ensued.

"Murderer! Come outside, you evil bitch!"

Tom was already at the window. "It's Benita. She's in the street."

We rushed onto the porch. The two officers Detective Lane had stationed outside were approaching 65-year-old Benita, who was waving her cane like a weapon. Her face was ravaged by grief, hair wild, clothes disheveled.

"My son is dead!" she screamed, her voice echoing down the quiet street. "You killed him! You killed my baby!"

"Ma'am, you need to calm down," one of the officers said, reaching for her arm.

She jerked away. "Don't touch me! That witch in there-" she pointed her cane at me, "-she took everything from me! Everything!"

I watched her collapse into tears, still screaming accusations, and felt my chest constrict. I knew that pain. That raw, primal agony of losing your child. Every morning I woke up without Benji felt like drowning.

"Benita," I called out, my voice shaking. "I'm so sorry about Gino. But I didn't-"

"Sorry?" She lunged forward, the officers barely catching her. "Sorry doesn't bring back my son!"

Those words hit me in ways she would never know.

"That's enough," Tom stepped in front of me.

"Ma'am, this is your final warning," the female officer said. "Leave now or we will arrest you."

Benita spat on the ground. "Arrest me! I don't care! I have nothing left to lose!" She tried to push past the officers. "You hear me, bitch? Nothing left to lose!"

"Please," Angelique whispered beside me. "Let's go inside."

But I couldn't move. I watched as Benita fought against the officers, her grief turning to rage, then back to grief. When they finally took her down, her wails filled the morning air.

"My son! My only son!" She thrashed as they cuffed her. "He was all I had! All I had!"

Tears streamed down my face. "Benji's all I have," I whispered.

They loaded her into the cruiser, her screams muffled behind the glass. As they drove away, her eyes locked with mine through the window. The hatred there made me stumble backward.

Tom guided me inside, Angelique following with the forgotten coffees. I sank onto the couch, shaking.

"You don't think..." I couldn't finish the sentence.

"Think what?" Angelique sat beside me.

"What if she took him? What if this whole time, Benji's been..." I pressed my hands to my mouth, choking back a sob.

Tom knelt in front of me. "We'll tell Detective Lane about this. If there's any connection-"

"She said she had nothing left to lose." The words felt like glass in my throat. "What if she took my baby to make me feel what she's feeling now? To make me lose everything too?"

Angelique wrapped her arms around me as I broke down. Outside, the neighborhood was quiet again, as if nothing had happened. As if a grieving mother hadn't just been arrested in the street. As if my son wasn't still missing.

As if all our broken hearts didn't matter at all.

Angelique grabbed my hands and began to pray. *"Father God in the name of Jesus..."* Her words soothed my ears as she cried out to God on my behalf that He would bring my son back to me safe and sound. I teared up because I felt every word, but when Angelique started praying for Benita too, I almost wanted to snatch my hands away. A selfish thought flashed through my mind that she didn't need prayer, she needed to leave me the hell alone, but I let it die. The woman had lost her son. Though it wasn't my fault, I understood her rage.

I would give anything to have Benji back just like she would do the same to bring back Gino. After the prayer, Angelique had to go to class, so Tom and I calmly waited for Detective Lane to arrive.

Chapter 15

Detective Lane arrived within the hour. "We're searching her house," he said. "I've got our best team on it."

"How long?" My voice sounded strange, stretched thin.

"A few hours, maybe more. We'll be thorough."

Tom tried to get me to eat something, to rest, to do anything but pace the floor watching the clock. But I couldn't stay still. Every minute felt like glass under my skin.

"He could be there," I kept saying. "All this time, he could have been there."

"Try to breathe," Tom said, but his own voice was tight with tension.

I watched the shadows move across the wall as morning became afternoon. The hope in my chest grew with each passing hour, becoming something wild and desperate. This had to be it. After a full month of searching, of praying, of dying inside - this had to be where we'd find him.

At three o'clock, Clara came by with Peter as she always did. "Hey Tee Tee!" Peter said, waving a piece of red construction paper in his hands.

Clara gave me a pained smile.

"What is this?" I asked, eyeing my friend before focusing on her son.

Clara tensed, but Peter burst with excitement as he told me. "I made you a picture." He beamed as he shared it with me. It was three figures surrounded by a heart. "That's me, you, and Benji," he said as he pointed. "We will give it to him when he comes home."

My eyes blurred with tears. I almost couldn't take it. Peter was such a sweet boy but he had no clue what his gesture had done to me.

"Thank you, baby," I croaked out, then kissed the top of his head so he wouldn't feel hurt by my emotional response. I hugged him tightly, then I imagined how I used to hug Benji and I broke down.

Clara came over to gently take her son and Tom held me.

"What's wrong, Tee Tee?" Peter asked, and Clara soothed him.

"Shhh, honey. She's fine. Remember how I told you that grown ups get upset sometimes? She's fine."

But I wasn't fine. I never would be until I had my son.

Detective Lane needed to hurry up.

Clara and Peter stayed for about an hour then they headed home.

Then it was just me and Tom waiting for Detective Lane once again.

When the knock finally came, I nearly tripped running to the door. My hands were shaking so badly I could barely turn the knob.

But it was just Detective Lane. Alone.

Another hole pierced through my heart.

"Where's Benji?" The words tumbled out before I could stop them. "Did you find him?"

The detective's face told me everything before he spoke. "I'm sorry, Nadine. We didn't find any evidence that Benji was ever there."

"No." I shook my head. "No, you have to look again. She must have hidden him somewhere-"

"We searched every inch. The basement, the attic, all the closets. We brought in dogs. There's no sign that Benji was ever in that house."

"But she threatened me! She said-"

"She was grief-stricken and angry. She wanted to hurt you, yes, but not..." He sighed. "She didn't take Benji."

My legs gave out. Tom caught me before I hit the floor, but I barely felt his arms around me. The hope that had been building all day shattered, leaving me hollow.

"My baby," I sobbed. "Where's my baby?"

Tom held me tighter, murmuring something I couldn't hear over my own crying. The floor was hard beneath my knees, but the pain didn't register. Nothing registered except this: another dead end. Another day without Benji.

"We're not giving up," Detective Lane said from somewhere above me. "We'll keep looking."

But his words sounded far away, meaningless. Because Benji wasn't at Benita's house. Benji wasn't coming home today.

And I was starting to wonder if he ever would.

Chapter 16

Tom tried to take my mind off Benji by taking me out for dinner and dancing, but I didn't want to go. I told him I couldn't go out for a night on the town while my son was God knows where with God knows who. Tom eventually wore me down and I agreed to go out to take my mind off things. When he went home, he said he would be back at seven to pick me up.

In the meantime, I forced myself to produce a badly written article to keep my job. My boss Dexter had been more than gracious with me, extending deadlines well beyond what he normally would have done, and he had also emailed and called me every week since Benji's disappearance to see how I was doing. I mustered up a draft and sent it to him, reasoning that the editor could fix it. I'd done all I could do.

Dexter wrote back thanking me for my submission and asked how I was doing. I didn't want to respond but kept it short and sweet and said that I was okay. It was a lie, but I was tired of being vulnerable in front of people. Tired of being powerless, weak, and desperate. All I wanted was my son. I wished I would have gotten him one of those trackers where you could find your kid anywhere they went. Hindsight was 20/20, but who could have predicted this?

Before I knew it, time had flown by and it was after six-thirty in the evening. I had less than half an hour to get ready for dinner with Tom. I rushed into the shower and threw a quick outfit together, arranging my hair in a stylish updo and applying minimalist makeup with a black dress I'd already worn but thought was still clean.

I gave myself a onceover in the mirror and felt like dirt. I was going out to dinner while my son was suffering? It was unforgiveable. But when I thought of how Tom had bent over backward for me since Benji went missing, I believed I owed it to him to at least pretend to be excited about tonight. I couldn't deny that I was a tiny bit excited. Before Benji's disappearance, Tom and I had shared chemistry that I secretly wanted to explore but was afraid to. I wondered if Tom felt it too. He never said he did, but I had a feeling. Maybe it was just a feeling. Maybe Tom saw me as nothing more than his younger sister's best friend.

After spraying two puffs of perfume, I was ready. A knock sounded at the front door and it was Tom, right on time. He was dressed nicely in dress pants, a button-down shirt, and he wore a nice watch. His beard was neatly trimmed and his mocha brown skin was blemish free. He pinned me with an intense gaze that made me nervous, but I forced myself not to blush. There was no time for romance while my son was out there, helpless and defenseless.

Tom extended his strong, muscular arm, and I took his hand. He led me off the porch and to his freshly washed and vacuumed car. It was gleaming in the moonlight. My breath caught in my throat at the thought that he did this to impress me but I tried not to read into it. Tom opened the passenger's side door and I slid inside while he closed it behind me. Without thinking, I reached across to open the driver's side door for him. Tom saw the gesture and smiled as he slid into his seat. I blushed but neither of us said anything.

Soft music played all the way to the Hooky Lounge, a vibey restaurant and dance floor that hosted singers, spoken word artists, and live musicians. I felt a rush of excitement when we pulled up because I had always wanted to visit this place. It was new - just opened within the past six months, and I had heard nothing but good things about it. My excitement lasted a couple of seconds before a wave of guilt took its place.

Tom was studying my profile. "You good?" he asked, and I nodded. We exited the vehicle and entered the restaurant to find a homey atmosphere. A jazz musician was playing a saxophone and low rumbles of chatter filled the room, which was a maze of tables half-full with diners. The hostess greeted us with a smile and led us to an empty table immediately, handing us each a menu before telling us our server would be with us shortly.

I studied the food selections and my mouth watered as the scent of fried catfish filled my nostrils. It smelled so good I wanted to find whoever ordered it and take it from their plate. I looked up from my menu at Tom and found him staring at me. My heart dropped as I felt a pang of guilt, and I quickly looked down.

"See anything you like?" Tom asked, and I looked up again. He was fixing me with that intense gaze again.

"Um... the fried catfish looks good," I said. Tom smiled, and for the first time, I noticed his perfectly white teeth. Tom and I had known each other forever with him being Clara's brother, but I never had the chance to really study him until tonight, despite our chemistry. I didn't know what changed – maybe the fact that he asked me out to dinner. It still could have been him just trying to be nice, but my heart told me his gesture meant more. His smooth-looking lips looked so inviting that I wanted to taste them along with the catfish but I caught myself. An image of Benji flashed in my mind and I straightened up.

"What are you ordering?" I asked in a business-like tone. Tom's gaze didn't wane.

"I'll go with the fried chicken," he replied.

The server came over and took our drink orders, then asked if we knew what we wanted for dinner. We told him our orders and he took our menus and walked away.

"You look beautiful tonight," Tom said, after the server was out of earshot. Those words made me nervous but I still replied.

"Thank you. You look great too."

Tom chuckled. "I clean up nicely, huh?"

An involuntary smile quirked across my lips. "Indeed, you do."

We were silent for a moment before Tom said, "This place is nice, huh?" I took in the environment. Soft lighting, the music, friendly staff, paintings of various blues, funk, and R&B musicians. I was impressed. "This place is a vibe," I said.

There was also a huge wall with markers attached by metallic cords that said, *Tell the world you've been here.* The board was filled with signatures of patrons who had visited since the restaurant opened six months ago. Under different circumstances, I would have been more excited to be here, but tonight I just couldn't. My interests were divided between Tom and Benji. Still, I forced a smile. "We have to sign the board when we leave," I gestured.

Tom turned and craned his neck to look, then turned back with a smile. "Indeed, we do."

The server returned with our drinks and I felt myself begin to relax for the first time in a long time. Was it Tom, the scent of the burning incense, or just the atmosphere? My first mind said it was Tom. He'd outdone himself to make sure I was good ever since my son was stripped away from me. I would never be able to repay him. I opened my mouth to say this, but the server came with our food.

"That was quick," I commented, and the server smiled.

"On busy nights like this, we keep certain dishes rolling," he said with a wink.

I believed him, based on the sight of the plate before me. My mouth watered. From the looks of it alone, the catfish was fried to perfection. So was Tom's chicken. Tom said Grace and we dove into our meals. I couldn't believe that not only was I eating, I actually wanted to. The catfish was so good I wanted to devour it, but also not burn my tongue in the process.

"Damn," Tom said after taking a bite of his chicken. "That's good."

I smiled and he grabbed another one of his drumsticks and extended it toward me. "Take a bite," he said. I was caught off guard, but Tom was grinning. I leaned forward and Tom watched as I took a tiny bite. The juicy, crunchy, well-seasoned meat was to die for.

"Wow, they're frying chicken like that?" I said. "The grandmothers of this city better watch out!"

Tom and I shared a laugh before I realized I had let my guard down. Was that a good thing or bad thing? I knew being perpetually stressed wasn't good. I decided to relax into this evening and pick my worries back up when I got back home. We enjoyed our meals and drinks, then Tom abruptly stood after wiping his hands with a napkin. He gestured for me to follow suit.

"Dance with me," he said. My prior nervousness returned. But since the night was a vibe, I obliged. I took Tom's waiting hand and allowed him to lead me to the dance floor. We found an open space and Tom wrapped his arms around my waist while my arms encircled his neck. We swayed back and forth to the saxophonist's melody.

I relaxed the more I swayed in his arms, inhaling his intoxicating masculine scent. I looked up into his eyes and Tom was already staring down at me.

How could I resist him so long?

Clara's brother was fine as hell.

I never thought I would be out on a date with Tom until tonight. With the way he was looking at me, like he wanted me, this wasn't some friendly gesture to take my mind off my son. I was ready to accept the fact that Tom wanted me just like I wanted him. I had been worried before that Clara might feel some type of way about me dating her brother, but she knew I was a good woman. If Tom and I were feeling each other, why not pursue it? The more I thought about it, the more right it felt.

Tonight was perfect in every way... Until I saw a flash of red and stopped in my tracks.

I almost choked at the sight of a man putting on a red windbreaker. It was just like the one from my nightmares, the jacket I remembered from the day Benji was taken from me.

"Hey!" I was screaming, before I realized it.

Tom was startled but caught on when I kicked off my heels and ran barefoot after the man who was leaving the restaurant. I practically tackled him in the parking lot until I realized there was no way that was the same jacket. It didn't have the same white stripe down the front as the one from my memories.

Shame coursed my veins. "I'm so sorry," I kept repeating while the tears ran down my face.

The man curled his lips at me in disgust while Tom stepped forward, clutching my heels and purse in his hands. "Sir, her son was kidnapped last month, and the person who took him was wearing a red jacket like yours," he explained, but the man wasn't trying to hear an explanation.

"You nearly gave me a heart attack, barreling down on me like a linebacker, young lady!"

Thoroughly ashamed, I apologized to the man once again, but he grunted in disapproval and left in a huff. There was nothing left to do but collapse into Tom's arms. He held me in the parking lot until I was able to calm from my raging emotions.

Chapter 17

Hanging by a thread had become my new normal. It had been two weeks since the restaurant fiasco. Tom didn't say anything about what happened when we got back to my place, which I was thankful for, but he also hadn't tried to get me to leave the house again since then. I wasn't sure how to feel about that part.

Since he had to return to his construction business, I was left alone during the day. Not that I minded, but I had gotten used to him sleeping on my couch and then us waking up in the morning with each other.

Either Tom or I would prepare breakfast, and we would chat about random things. I knew Tom mostly did it to keep my mind off Benji, and I was grateful for it.

Since he had gone back to work, I spent my days forcing sentences across pages for my backed up list of articles I needed to produce. It was the only thing holding me back from insanity. If I didn't still have this job, I probably would have slit my wrists by now.

The pain was too intense.

I would not wish it on anyone.

After forcing the words to another mediocre article, I sent it to Dexter and turned off my computer. I didn't want to wait for his reply because it had been his routine to ask at least once a week how I was doing.

I fixed myself a half a sandwich, then ate that while surfing through channels on television. It was ten in the morning, so there were six more hours until Tom came home. He was still living between my place and his own, but mostly my place because the only things he did at home were shower and change, then come back to me.

Heat rose to my cheeks at that thought, because I still felt chemistry between me and Tom even after the restaurant fiasco, but I let the feeling die out.

Grabbing my phone, I decided to re-activate my social media profile so I could see the messages people had left on my timeline about Benji. Though I never shared this with anyone, I often looked back at the messages just to see the kind words from parents of Benji's classmates and teammates, as well as friends and acquaintances who had met my son or heard the news of his abduction and expressed their concerns.

I scrolled through the messages as if seeing them for the first time, tears welling in my eyes like they usually did.

Some of them were heartfelt prayers and others were just kind words, but either way, it felt good to know that people spoke such positivity about my son.

After an hour of scrolling, I'd had enough for the day.

I went to the main timeline screen and was about to close out the app when an image caught my eye.

Second Grade Science Fair Wows the Mayor, the caption read.

But I wasn't caught up on the caption. My eyes zeroed in on one of the little boys in the photo. I blinked rapidly as my heart rate raised, then I enlarged the photo to ensure that I hadn't officially lost my mind.

I hadn't.

I was staring at the smiling face of my son, who was standing behind a small table that held a volcano he'd made.

It was unbelievable.

"Benji?" I said aloud, fearful that I was daydreaming. Then I enlarged the photo again. It was him. Wearing one of his favorite dinosaur shirts, though I could have sworn that one was still hanging in his closet.

It couldn't be Benji, could it?

I clicked on the link to the attached article, and there the photo was again, along with several single photos of the children who had participated in the science fair.

I scrolled til I saw the boy who looked like Benji and my heart dropped.

My breath caught in my throat. *Benjamin shows off his award-winning volcano,* the caption read.

Gasping, I clapped my hand over my lips. "Benji!" I let out in a strangled tone. "Benji!"

Benji participated at a science fair in Connecticut? There was no way.

My hands trembled so badly I almost dropped the phone. I forced myself to take several screenshots, afraid the post might disappear. Each breath came in sharp gasps as I studied every pixel of his face. That slight dimple in his left cheek when he smiled. The way he cocked his head to the left when he posed. This wasn't just a look-alike - this was my baby.

My first instinct was to call Detective Lane, but my fingers hovered over his number. The police had been useless so far. What if they took too long to act? What if they scared away whoever had him before I could get to him? My heart was hammering so hard I could hear my pulse in my ears. No, I couldn't risk losing him again.

I paced the living room, my thoughts racing faster than my feet could carry me.

Then in a snap judgement, I swiped my screen and found Detective Lane's number in my contacts. I pressed the green button and let it ring until it went to voicemail. His voice came on the line for me to leave a message, but I was done waiting on the police. Hanging up, I continued to pace the floor.

Benji was in Connecticut. I had all the information I needed to go get him. Why not just go?

A few weeks ago, I'd been ready to give up. The darkness had been suffocating, crushing, absolute. But now? That spark of hope burned through everything else, setting my nerve endings on fire. I couldn't just stand here twiddling my thumbs and waiting for the detective to call me back. I couldn't think straight. My son was alive. My son was in Connecticut. My son needed me.

"I'm coming, baby," I whispered, my voice cracking. The fog of depression that had weighed me down lifted like smoke in a strong wind. My hands were still shaking, but not from fear anymore - from determination. I tried to steady myself enough to think clearly. Should I call Tom? Clara or Angelique?

No. Every minute I waited was another minute my son was with whoever took him. I could feel my maternal instincts taking over, that primal need to protect overriding everything else. The same force that would make a mother lift a car off her child was pushing me toward the door.

I grabbed my purse, nearly knocking over a lamp in my haste. My fingers fumbled with my coat buttons as adrenaline coursed through my veins. I could barely focus enough to find my car keys. The rational part of my brain was screaming at me to slow down, to think this through, to call someone - anyone. But the mother in me? She was already halfway to Connecticut.

I checked the name of the school. Fairview Elementary in Sawsucket Connecticut. That was two hours from where I was in Ridgeview Massachusetts.

This was why we couldn't find my son. Someone had taken him to Connecticut. My nose wrinkled. Who the hell did I know in Connecticut? No one.

Someone from Benita's family?

I wasn't sure, but I would damn sure find out.

With a renewed vigor that grew by the moment, I raced out the door and cranked up my engine to head to Connecticut.

Chapter 18

I was on the highway in what felt like seconds. At first, I was riding off pure adrenaline, then about forty five minutes into my drive, my rational mind kicked in. What if it wasn't safe? I was using my GPS to navigate to the school like all I had to do was pull up, get out of the car, and demand answers, but would it be that simple?

I should tell someone where I am, I thought. I wasn't familiar with Sawsucket. Though I'd been to Connecticut plenty of times, I had never traveled that far into the state. Who knew what awaited me there?

Pulling over onto a shoulder, I sent a quick group text to Tom, Clara, and Angelique to let them know what was going on. *I found Benji!* I texted, not believing the words I was typing. I also sent them one of the screenshots I had taken from the article.

Headed to CT now.

That message should have sufficed, I thought. It should have been enough to let them know that I wasn't crazy and that I had indeed found Benji. Once they saw his photo, they would know why I had to leave immediately.

It had been far too long without my son.

My dashboard immediately began blowing up with notifications from Tom and my friends, to the point that their messages were crowding my GPS screen. I quickly tapped to dismiss them, then disabled all text notifications.

Minutes later, a call came through my Bluetooth from Tom.

"Hello?" I answered, a giddy feeling sweeping through me.

Tom spoke in a tentative tone. "Nadine, where are you?"

I giggled, realization dawning on me more and more. "I'm on my way to Connecticut. Did you see my text? I found him!"

Tom was silent for a few moments before he sighed. "Nadine, where in Connecticut are you going?"

"Sawsucket."

"Saw... Nadine, wait. Turn around. This isn't right," he urged.

I tensed. "What do you mean it's not right, Tom? Did you not see the photo I sent?"

He spoke in a calm but assertive tone. "Yes, I saw the photo and it does look like Benji, but we aren't sure of that, Nadine. We need to think this through."

My exit was in twenty miles.

"There's nothing to think about, Tom. I need to see my son."

"Na..."

I ended the call.

Tom tried to call back, but I declined it, determination coursing my veins. I was going to get my son and nothing was stopping me.

Eighteen more miles.

A few minutes after that, Detective Lane called my phone, but I declined that too, snorting when I saw that he left a voicemail.

"Oh, now he wants to call me," I mocked. I spent almost two months being without my son and waited on his so-called detective work, and Benji was in Connecticut this whole time.

If Detective Lane wanted to talk to me, he could meet me at my destination.

Ten miles left.

More calls came in, but I declined them one by one.

Angelique.

Declined.

Clara.

Declined.

Tom again.

Declined.

A tiny voice in the back of my mind whispered that Tom might be right - that I should slow down, think this through. But that voice was drowned out by the memory of Benji's empty bed, his untouched dinosaur shirt, the silence in our home where his laughter used to be.

Nothing was taking me away from my son, not when I was so close.

My hands were white-knuckled on the steering wheel. Each declined call made my heart race faster, but I couldn't let anyone talk me out of this. Not when I was so close. My mouth was dry, and I realized I hadn't taken a single sip of water since leaving home.

Five miles away.

I would need a hotel, I reasoned. I might need to stay here a few days until I figured out what was going on. Would Benji be at the school?

I checked the time. It was around noon, so they would probably be eating lunch soon.

I could not wait to see his face, to hold him and hug him and tell him how much I missed him.

Another call came through from Detective Lane just as I was taking the exit to Sawsucket.

Declined.

I would get back to him later once I got my son back. Then he could help me throw whoever took him behind bars and we could throw away the key together.

The elementary school was ten minutes from the exit.

The familiar Massachusetts highways had given way to unknown Connecticut roads. Street names I'd never seen before. Buildings that held no memories. But somewhere in this strange town, my son was waiting.

What would I do if someone tried to stop me? If whoever took him was there? I had no plan, no weapon, nothing but my determination. But for Benji, I would face anything.

It seemed surreal to be so close to my son, when I felt so far away over these past two months.

Finally, I pulled up across the street from the school. My car was facing the playground and from the looks of it, they had just let the kids out for recess.

Chapter 19

Now that I was across the street from the elementary school, this no longer felt real. How could Benji be at this school? It was practically the middle of the school year. How would they transfer his records without no one knowing? They would have had to change his identity. But the article said Benjamin. Benji's name was Benjamin.

I pulled out my phone again to re-scrutinize the image.

My hands were shaking so badly I had to rest them against the car to steady them enough to look at the photo. Sweat beaded on my forehead despite the cool air, and my stomach churned with a mixture of hope and fear.

The playground was filled with children's laughter, a sound that used to fill my own home. Through the fence, I could see groups of kids playing tag, others on the swings. Each flash of movement drew my attention, making my heart skip a beat. Was that him? That one?

I probably looked like a crazy woman standing across the street from an elementary school, leaning against my car, staring at my phone, then at the kids, but I needed to know I wasn't crazy.

I took a step forward, then stepped back again. Maybe I should drive around to the front entrance and ask to speak with the principal. The principal could make an announcement over the intercom and someone could bring my son to me.

I reached for my door handle, but stopped myself again.

Had the photo been a figment of my imagination?

I checked again.

It wasn't.

I was staring right at it, and it was the same one I'd seen earlier. The one that made me take the trip to Sawsucket Connecticut.

A call from Clara came through, blocking my view of the photo temporarily. My finger smashed the Answer button.

"What?" I answered in a frustrated tone.

"Nadine?" she said breathlessly. "Where are you?"

I responded through gritted teeth. "I already told you, Connecticut. Stop calling my phone," I said roughly. "I'm trying to get my son!"

"Nadine, you're not thinking clearly," she said. "That's not Benji..."

"Yes it is Benji!" I thundered, just as a car rode by blasting music. Some of the kids from the playground looked in my direction and I instantly felt embarrassed.

"Look, I'll call you right back."

"Nadine, Detective Lane is coming out there..."

"Let him come then."

CLICK.

I ended the call.

My feelings were slightly hurt by the fact that no one seemed to believe in me despite the fact that they had seen Benji's photo, but fuck them. I knew my son. I had birthed him. I had seen him in that photo with my own eyes. Seen his name written in the caption. They might not have believed it, but I had my proof.

Now I was back to staring at the photo one more time to be sure it was Benji. Despite the fact that I'd just reamed out my best friend before hanging up on her, I wasn't entirely sure I was right. A thought flashed through my mind that I might finally be losing my sanity because I kept switching my convictions back and forth by the second, but I pushed it away.

Enlarging the photo, I studied it again from all angles to be sure I hadn't missed something.

Relief coursed my veins when I realized I was right.

It was Benji. I didn't know how they were able to get him into this school, but it was my son. Everything about him was the same, down to the haircut. The smile, even the outfit. Benji had that same shirt hanging in his closet... wait, how did they get the shirt? Did someone break into the house?

I thought back. Benji had been wearing a hoodie when he was taken, but what shirt was he wearing underneath? Had I let him wear the dinosaur shirt that day? It was possible. I hadn't checked his closet to verify before I left for Connecticut.

Part of me knew I should wait for Detective Lane. The rational part that understood procedures and protocols. But that part was being drowned out by the mother in me, the one who had spent countless nights staring at Benji's empty bed. How could any mother just stand here and wait?

The voicemail notification from Detective Lane was blinking on my phone. Sucking my teeth, I held down the number 1 on my keypad to listen to it.

After entering my password, the message began to play. *"Ms. Wilson, this is Detective Lane,"* he began in a

106

calm but assertive tone, much like Tom's had been. *"I received several phone calls from your friends saying that you believe you found Benji in Sawsucket Connecticut. I'm sending this message to tell you to hold off before trying to confront anyone or approach the boy. Please wait for me to arrive so we can sort this out. I..."*

I tuned out the rest of his words.

He called Benji *the boy* like he was some random kid and not my child who had been stripped away from me for two months. Detective Lane could come to Connecticut, but by that time, he might be too late. The kids were outside now. Maybe Benji was amongst them. I stepped forward, but stepped back again. What if Detective Lane was right? What if I didn't wait for him and I tried to take Benji, and then it somehow blew up in my face? I needed to be calm. I needed to think this through.

Taking a few short breaths, I developed a quick plan. Since I was standing right across from the kids at recess, it wouldn't hurt to take a closer look. All I needed to do was take a peek and see if Benji was there, and if he was, I would quietly leave and wait until Detective Lane got in town. I could check into a hotel while he was on his way and we could sort out a plan for how to get my son.

I took a deep breath. "Proceed with caution, Nadine," I urged myself.

Pacing myself was best in this situation because who knew what I would encounter if I did spot Benji? Nodding, my mind was made up. I would cross the street and take a closer look at the kids to see if Benji was indeed at this school, and once I determined that he was, I would fall back and let the Detective do his job.

In a few short hours, Benji would be home.

Chapter 20

I looked both ways to make sure there were no cars coming, then took a tentative step into the street. Then another.

I continued until I was standing in front of the gate, watching the children run and play across the huge playground that spanned the entire length of the school.

So many children were present.

Could any of them be Benji?

One of them had to be, unless he was absent.

A fleeting thought ran through my mind. What if the picture was old?

It couldn't have been, because Benji was taken only a month ago, but I whipped out my phone again just to be sure.

As I thought, the picture was taken a week ago.

I relaxed.

I wasn't crazy.

My son was at this school and I would be reunited with him soon, I could feel it.

Fingering the gate, I scanned the sea of children. Little boys and girls of various ages, with teachers standing watch. A smile curved onto my lips.

Benji loved recess.

My eyes swept across the playground methodically, not wanting to miss a single child. A group of boys playing soccer. Two girls on the monkey bars. A cluster of kids drawing with chalk near the basketball court.

Then I saw him.

The world tilted on its axis as my heart thumped in my chest. He was standing by the slide, wearing a blue t-shirt, laughing with another boy. That laugh. I would know that laugh anywhere. My legs went weak, and I had to grab the fence to stay upright.

Before I could process what I was doing, my feet were moving. I found the gate, fumbling with the latch with trembling fingers. It swung open with a metallic screech that was lost in the sounds of children playing.

My walk became a run. Teachers turned their heads in my direction, but I barely registered their presence. All I could see was my son, alive and whole and right there in front of me.

"Benji!" The name tore from my throat. "Benji!"

He turned at my voice, and time seemed to slow down. His eyes met mine, but instead of recognition, there was only confusion. It didn't matter. Nothing mattered except reaching him.

I crashed to my knees in front of him, wrapping my arms around his small frame. He was real. Solid. Warm. Tears streamed down my face as I pulled him close, breathing in his scent.

"Oh God, Benji, I found you. I found you!"

But something was wrong. The body in my arms was rigid, unresponsive.

Was he rejecting me? Why was Benji acting so stiff? Was he not happy to see me? Had he already forgotten about me?

And then I heard it – a small, frightened, tentative voice:

"Mommy?"

I slowly pulled back and stared into his little brown eyes.

"What is it, honey?" I studied him intently, desperate for answers, but only saw confusion.

Chapter 21

"Baby, are you okay? Did they hurt you?" I pulled back to examine his face, running my hands over his arms, his shoulders, checking for any signs of injury.

He stared at me with wide, scared eyes, trying to pull away.

My heart lurched. "Benji, it's Mommy. Don't you recognize me?"

"Ms. Thompson!" Benji called out, his voice trembling.

A teacher in a navy cardigan rushed over, her sensible shoes crunching against the playground gravel. "What's going on here?" Her tone was sharp but controlled, practiced in the way of someone used to handling difficult situations with children present.

She stared between me and Benji, her face etched in the same confusion as my son.

"Are you okay?" she asked, as if I were the one who was crazy in this situation.

I whirled on her, still keeping one hand on Benji's shoulder. "How dare you! How could you enroll my son in this school without questioning anything? He was kidnapped! His face was all over the news, and you just let someone walk in here and register him?"

The teacher's face shifted from concern to confusion. "Ma'am, I don't know what you're talking about." She looked at Benji, then at me again. "I don't understand what's happening, but I think you need to step away from Benjamin."

"Step away? Step away?" My voice rose hysterically. "This is my son! Someone took him from me, and you people just—"

"Please," she cut in firmly, gesturing to another teacher across the playground. "Mrs. Rodriguez, could you watch the children?" Then she turned back to me, lowering her voice. "We should continue this conversation inside. Now."

"I'm not going anywhere without my son."

"Ma'am." Her voice was steel wrapped in velvet. "Either we handle this calmly inside the building, or I'll have no choice but to call the police."

Benji was trembling under my hand now, and something about his reaction made my stomach twist. I looked down at him, really looked at him, and for the first time, a sliver of doubt crept in.

But I couldn't be wrong, right? This was Benji, my baby.

What was happening?

The teacher's stance remained firm, her arms crossed over her chest and her lips forming a straight line.

"Fine," I said, my voice hoarse. "Let's go inside."

The teacher nodded, then spoke softly to Benji. "Benjamin, honey, why don't you go play with your friends while us grown ups have a discussion?"

"No!" I protested. "My son stays with me!"

But Benji was already backing away, nearly tripping over his feet in his haste to join a group of boys by the basketball court. The sight of him running from me felt like a physical blow.

A few steps toward the boys however, and Benji stopped short. He slowly turned around, a worried look on his face, then he ran back toward me, grabbing my hand.

My heart swarmed with joy.

The teacher gestured toward the school building. "This way, please." Her tone made it clear this wasn't a request.

I followed her, my legs wooden, my mind racing. Something wasn't right. But what? The photo, the face, the dinosaur shirt – it was all exactly like Benji. Wasn't it?

As we walked toward the building, I could hear the resumed sounds of children playing behind us, as if nothing had happened.

As if my world wasn't falling apart all over again.

Chapter 22

We entered a small second grade classroom, judging from the huge sign on the door. A woman was sitting at the desk staring into space and eating lunch, but she looked up like a deer in headlights when she saw me, Ms. Thompson, and Benji.

"Ms. Thompson? What's—" She froze mid-sentence, her eyes widening as they locked onto me.

"Ms. Marshall," the recess teacher said carefully, "Benjamin's mother has some concerns that she needs to address with you. I thought it best for you two to speak in private, but she insisted that Benjamin come inside with her."

Ms. Marshall didn't seem to be following the conversation. "...Okay...?"

Ms. Thompson nodded, took one more look at me and Benji, then exited the classroom to go back outside.

I faced Ms. Marshall. "I'm calling the police right now," I announced, pulling out my phone. "My son has been missing for over two months, and somehow he ends up enrolled at your school?"

Ms. Marshall's head snapped back in shock, then she stood up so quickly her chair scraped against the floor. "Wait, why are you calling the police? That's not..."

But I was already dialing, my fingers shaking with rage. Detective Lane picked up on the second ring.

"Detective Lane, I found him. I found Benji. He's here at Sawsucket Elementary School."

"Ms. Wilson?" His voice crackled through the speaker. "You're actually at the school now?"

"Yes, and he's right here in front of me! They have him enrolled here like nothing happened. Like he wasn't kidnapped!"

"That's..." Detective Lane paused. "That's impossible. Are you absolutely certain—"

"Of course I'm certain! When will you get here?"

"I'm still about an hour out with this traffic. I'll try to send some officers ahead of me. They can probably be there in twenty minutes. Don't do anything until—"

"An hour? No, I need someone here now! I want to know who enrolled my son in this school!"

Ms. Marshall stepped forward, her hands raised in a placating gesture. "Please, Deenie, just calm down and—"

I froze, my phone nearly slipping from my grip. "What did you just call me?"

"Deenie," she repeated softly. "That's your name."

The room tilted sideways. Nobody called me Deenie. Why was she saying that name confidently like she knew me? I held the phone away from my ear and stared at the teacher in shock while Detective Lane was still talking on the other end of the phone. My mouth opened to respond, but before I could form words, the door swung open.

An older woman who I presumed to be the principal stood in the doorway, her expression grave.

116

Chapter 23

The principal's eyes darted between us, her professional composure slipping. "Ladies?" The word hung in the air like a question mark. "May I ask what's going on?"

I didn't know what the hell these people's problem was, but I was sick of this situation already. My hands were shaking so badly I could barely end the call with Detective Lane. Sweat trickled down my spine as I faced the principal.

"I'm taking my son home right now." The words came out raw, my throat so dry I could barely speak. I reached for Benji, who shrank back against Ms. Marshall's desk.

The principal nodded calmly. "Of course, Ms. Price. We just need you to sign him out at the front office—"

"Ms. Price?" I repeated, puzzled that she called me by a different name, but I let that go and focused on the matter at hand. "Why aren't you more concerned about this?" My chest tightened, each breath coming faster than the last. The fluorescent lights seemed too bright, the room too small. "Why are you acting like this is normal?"

I turned to Benji, my vision blurring at the edges. He was watching me with those same frightened eyes. "Baby, did they hurt you? What did they do to you?" My heart hammered against my ribs so hard I thought it might burst. "No, don't answer that. Wait for the police. You need to tell everything to the police."

"The police?" The principal's brow furrowed. "What on earth is going on here?"

"My son was kidnapped!" I gripped the edge of a nearby desk, my knuckles turning white, trying to anchor myself as the room tilted sideways. "He's been missing for over two months, and somehow he ends up here, in your school, in a different state!"

The principal exchanged a bewildered look with Ms. Marshall. "Ms. Price, I don't know what's going on, but I can assure you that no one has taken your son. As you can see, he's right here. Didn't you drop him off this morning?"

My stomach lurched. The metallic taste of fear filled my mouth as the room seemed to spin. "Stop calling me Ms. Price!" My voice cracked like thin ice. "My name is Nadine Wilson, and no, I didn't drop him off this morning! I haven't seen my son in over two months until today! Again, why are you all acting like this is normal?"

Benji pressed himself further against the wall, his lower lip trembling. "Mom," he whispered, "you're scaring me."

But the way he said *Mom* – the pitch was right, the voice was his, but the inflection was all wrong. My Benji always drew out the 'o' sound, made it warmer somehow. This was sharp, frightened, foreign.

I had practically flown here from Massachusetts as soon as I saw Benji's picture, but now that he was standing right here with me, all my confidence was slowly dwindling. Something wasn't right.

118

Chapter 24

For a few long moments, we all stared at each other, none of us knowing what to say or how to handle this situation. *This is why you should have waited for Detective Lane,* my mind reasoned, but who knew they all would try to play mind games on me like this? The whole school? The teacher and the principal were in on it? What the hell was happening?

Thankfully, help arrived less than two minutes later.

"Officers Rodriguez and Chen," a female officer announced as they entered the classroom. "We received a call about a possible child abduction situation?"

"There's been a huge misunderstanding," the principal started, her wrinkled face reddening. "Ms. Price dropped Benjamin off this morning, like she always does, and then she returned acting... well, confused."

She turned to look at me as if I had exhibited psychotic symptoms.

"That's not true!" I interjected. "I haven't dropped my son off anywhere in two months because he was taken from me!"

Officer Chen pulled out his notepad. "Let's just calm down and get everyone's statement—"

The door opened again. The secretary poked her head in first. "Sorry to interrupt, but Benjamin's mother is here with his lunch, and—" The secretary looked at me and did a double take. Her jaw dropped in shock, then her head whipped toward someone behind her.

A woman walked into the room, clutching a Ninja Turtle lunch box. She stopped dead in her tracks, the lunch box slipping from her fingers and hitting the floor with a clatter that seemed to echo through the suddenly silent room.

I stared at her. She stared at me.

It was like looking in a mirror.

We had the same face. The same hair. The same everything.

The room started to spin.

Everyone's eyes bounced between us like they were watching some bizarre tennis match. Same height. Same build. Same braided updo. Same high cheekbones and deep brown eyes.

"I knew it!" Benji's voice cut through the tension. He stepped forward, his fear forgotten in the face of discovery. "Your marks are different!"

My hand flew to my left cheek automatically, touching the small dark beauty mark that had been there since birth. Across from me, my double's fingers mirrored my movement, but to her right cheek.

"What the hell is going on?" we said simultaneously, then stared at each other in horror at the synchronicity.

"You—" I started.

"How are you—" she began.

"Ladies," the principal interrupted, holding up both hands. "I can hear the children coming in from recess. We need to move this... discussion... somewhere more private." She glanced at the officers, who nodded in agreement. "The conference room would be better."

"I don't understand," my double whispered, still staring at me like she was seeing a ghost. "This isn't possible."

"Ms. Price— uh, both of you," the principal corrected herself, "please. This way."

Benji picked up the fallen lunch box and handed it to... to the other me. His real mother? The thought made my stomach lurch.

"You can stay here, Benny," the other woman said, handing him back the lunch box, and I froze.

Benny? Did she just call him Benny?

"But..." My vision blurred. What was happening to me? What was this? Who was this woman and how did she get my son?

He's not Benji, my gut said, but my heart didn't want to listen.

Kneeling down to Benji's eye level, I quickly checked behind his ears. No birthmark.

My jaw dropped in shock as realization dawned. Benji had a birthmark in the shape of a crescent moon. This boy had no birthmark behind his ear.

I gently rubbed behind both ears while the other adults stared at me in bewildered silence until my eyes blurred once again. This was no coverup.

This boy was not my Benji.

A sob escaped my lips.

"Benji!" I choked out, but the boy grabbed his mother's hand.

"It's Benny!" he said, confidence etched in his tone.

I sank in defeat and the woman gave me a wistful smile as if she understood me, though I knew there was no way she could.

Benny went to his seat as the rest of his classmates filed in.

As I followed the principal, secretary, the woman, and the two police officers out of the classroom, I could hear the growing chorus of children's voices in the hallway. Everything felt surreal, like I was moving through a dream. Or a nightmare.

The last thing I saw before the classroom door closed was Benny watching us leave, his face a mixture of confusion and fascination, as if he'd just discovered the answer to a puzzle he didn't even know existed.

Chapter 25

I had never been more confused in my life. My steps were hollow as I followed my lookalike, the principal, the secretary, and the two police officers down the long hallway.

The conference room felt too small for all the questions expanding between us. We sat across from each other, mirror images in matching poses of disbelief.

"When's your birthday?" we asked simultaneously, then let out nervous laughs.

"September 15th," I said.

"1994," she finished, her eyes widening. "Where were you born?"

"St. Mary's Hospital in—"

"Ridgeview Massachusetts," she completed.

We stared at each other.

"But that's impossible," she said. "I wasn't adopted. My parents—"

"Neither was I. Though..." I swallowed hard. "My parents passed away ten years ago in a car accident."

"I'm Deenie," she offered softly. "Well, Nadeen Price, but everyone calls me Deenie."

"Nadine Wilson," I whispered. "Just... Nadine."

We continued asking each other questions and the more time wore on, the more stunned I became.

What. The hell. Is happening?

The door opened, and Detective Lane walked in, stopping short. His mouth opened and closed twice before he found his voice. "Well... this is unexpected."

I could tell from the way he was looking at me that he thought I had lost my damn mind just like Clara, Tom, and Angelique had. I almost wanted to give him a triumphant grin, until I thought about the fact that now that I had stumbled upon such a shocking discovery, I was in fact about to lose my damn mind.

How the fuck...?

Detective Lane cleared his throat and sat further down the table, still staring from me to Deenie, and back again.

I realized he was trying to tell us apart. I raised my hand. "I'm Nadine," I said. "Benji's mother. And she's..." My eyes clouded as I gestured toward the other woman. "She's Deenie, Benny's mother."

Detective Lane's face held a neutral expression, but his eyes told a different story. His eyes told me he thought what was happening was just as wild as I thought it was, though he wouldn't voice it.

That observation gave me a small sense of comfort, though my heart still ached for answers.

Deenie and I shared a glance, then we explained what little we knew, our words overlapping as we described discovering our identical appearances, same birthday, same hospital.

"A DNA test would confirm it," Detective Lane said, his voice sounding like he was fighting to regain control of this bizarre situation. He had probably thought he was coming to this school to talk me off a ledge, maybe even get me evaluated and thrown in some institution, but nothing could have prepared any of us for this. I agreed with his suggestion for the DNA test, though we all knew

125

it was just a formality. The evidence was written in our matching faces.

The afternoon slipped away as we shared fragments of our lives, trying to piece together this impossible puzzle. Deenie and I share the same peanut allergy. Same left-handedness. Same tendency to talk with our hands when excited.

When the final school bell rang, reality crashed back in. I felt untethered, lost in this strange mirror world where another me existed.

"You should head back home," Detective Lane suggested gently. "I can have your car towed, give you a ride—"

"No," I said quickly, then softened my tone. "I want to do the DNA test. I need to know for sure." Even though I already knew. I could feel it in my bones, in the way we finished each other's sentences, in how our gestures mirrored each other without trying.

"We can do it first thing tomorrow," Deenie said. She hesitated, then added, "I have a guest room. You should stay with us tonight."

The offer stunned me. She was willing to let me into her house?

One of the holes that were stabbed into my heart at Benji's disappearance slowly started to heal. This woman who just met me today, but who I had apparently been connected to my whole life, was willing to open her home and let me stay the night. She didn't have to do that. She could have seen me as some crazy woman and immediately demanded that I be hauled far away from her and her son, but she didn't. I could tell from Deenie's eyes that she shared my confusion, and she wanted answers too.

But should I stay at her house though?

Part of me wanted to refuse – it was too strange, too raw. But another part couldn't bear to leave. Even knowing her Benny wasn't my Benji, the resemblance pulled at my heart.

"Thank you," I managed.

Detective Lane shared a look with Deenie and she held a straight face but blushed when he looked away.

I didn't know how I managed, but I followed Deenie and Benny to their home while Detective Lane followed. Once we were inside, we all chatted for a few moments before Detective Lane said he was leaving but he would set up the DNA test for us.

Later that night, at Deenie's house – a craftsman-style home with blue shutters – my twin led me to the guest room. "Here," she said, pulling out a pair of pajamas. "They should fit."

I recognized them instantly – soft gray cotton with tiny stars. The same ones sitting in my drawer at home.

"Of course you have these," I said with a weak laugh. "I have the same ones at home." I stared down at the pajamas, then back up at Deenie with eyes full of tears.

Deenie smiled, but her eyes were serious. "We'll figure this out, Nadine. Whatever this is, we'll figure it out together."

I nodded, throat tight. As she left the room, I sat on the edge of the bed, holding the familiar-yet-not pajamas. Somewhere out there, my Benji was still missing. But somehow, impossibly, I'd found a sister I never knew existed.

Sleep would be impossible tonight.

Chapter 26

Now that I had a few moments to myself, my mind started scrambling again. How could I find the words to begin to describe what happened to me today? I had started the day off determined to find my missing son but ended up stumbling across my twin sister who apparently was somehow separated from me at birth. To add salt to the wound, her son looked just like my son. Benny and Benji could be twins, just like me and Deenie.

Sitting on the guest bed, I stared at my phone, trying to find the right words for Tom, Clara, and Angelique, who I knew all had to be sick with worry over me.

Finally, I typed: *Found something unexpected. I'm safe, but it wasn't Benji. There's a boy who looks exactly like him, but he has a mother who looks exactly like me. Same birthday, same hospital. Getting a DNA test tomorrow. Will explain more after. Please don't call - I need time to process this.*

I hit Send and watched the responses flood in immediately.

Tom: *What the hell?*

Clara: *OMG WHAT?*

Angelique: *ANSWER YOUR PHONE RIGHT NOW!*

My phone buzzed with incoming calls. I declined them all, sending another quick text:

I promise I'm okay. Just need space tonight. Will call tomorrow. I almost added that I was staying at Deenie's house tonight too, but I didn't. That would really make them blow their lids. I could already see Tom driving out here to get me and bring me back home.

I shook my head. It was better that they didn't know, at least for now.

Turning off my notifications, I set the phone face-down on the nightstand. The pajamas Deenie gave me felt familiar against my skin, but everything else felt surreal.

I tossed and turned for a few hours, watching the shadows of cars as their headlights flashed across the blinds sporadically, until my eyelids grew heavy from exhaustion and I fell asleep.

Morning came too quickly. I followed the scent of coffee and bacon to the kitchen, where Deenie stood at the stove in a robe identical to one I'd left at home.

"Morning," she said, glancing over her shoulder. "Coffee's fresh."

"Thanks." I found the mugs without having to ask which cabinet they were in. Of course they'd be there.

Benny bounded into the kitchen, already dressed for school. He stopped short when he saw me, then grinned. "Hi, Other Mom."

My chest tightened at his casual acceptance of this impossible situation. Deenie set a plate of scrambled eggs in front of him.

"Are eggs your favorite breakfast?" she asked me. There was a hint of amusement mixed with curiosity in her eyes and for a second, I grew excited too at the striking similarities between us.

I nodded. "With—"

"Bell peppers, onions, and cheese?"

My jaw dropped in awe as a chill went down my spine. This was getting scary how similar me and this woman were.

Deenie giggled, then said. "It's weird, right? How we're so similar?"

My eyes clouded, but I nodded.

She loaded up my plate with food, handed it to me, then said, "I was up half the night reading about twin studies. I'm actually a writer for a research magazine, so..."

I almost dropped my plate. This was too much.

"You write for a magazine too?"

Deenie's mouth fell open. "Yes, Everyday Insights," she said.

I was familiar with the name of the online magazine, though I'd never read it.

"I write for Style & Scenes."

Deenie's eyes widened. "I've heard of that magazine!"

"I've heard of yours too," I said softly.

We ate in awkward silence punctuated by Benny's chatter about his upcoming math test. I kept catching Deenie watching me when she thought I wasn't looking, and I knew I was doing the same.

Deenie broke the silence. "As I was saying earlier Nadine, our story isn't as uncommon as you think."

I stopped mid-bite and stared at her.

She quickly backtracked. "Wait... of course, this situation is different, but identical twins who were reared apart meeting each other for the first time often experience exactly what we experienced yesterday."

My mind was swimming. "They do?"

She nodded eagerly. "I found a ton of stories. Get this: There were these twin brothers born in Ohio who were separated at birth and lived 40 miles apart from each other their whole lives."

"Why were they separated?" Benny asked, his eyes full of intrigue.

I had the same question, but Deenie shook her head. "I'm not sure about that part, baby." She focused back on me. "But anyway, this was crazy: their adoptive parents named them both James. They both smoked the same brand of cigarettes. Both drove the same type of car, vacationed at the same beach in Florida, and both had the nickname Jim!"

My jaw dropped at this news, not believing my ears.

Benny cut in again. "But Other Mom doesn't have a nickname. Right?" He looked at me for confirmation.

"No, I don't," I said, a faint smile crossing my lips at my sister's astute son. He reminded me so much of Benji it hurt.

Deenie continued. "Those weren't the only similarities. Both twins had a childhood pet dog named Toy, they both liked math and hated reading, they both worked jobs in security, and here's the kicker: they both married a woman named Linda, only to divorce her and marry a woman named Betty."

My eyes widened. "What the f..." I stopped myself from cussing in front of my sister's son.

"Wow..." Benny said, just as amazed as me and Deenie.

"And they named their sons the same first and middle name," she finished softly.

That brought the excitement down a little for me. Half the reason I was sitting at this table was the fact that Deenie's son's name was Benjamin, just like Benji.

Deenie covered my hand with hers, then turned to her son.

"Time for school, buddy." She smiled at me again, then cleared our plates.

In the car, Benny sat in the back seat, humming to himself. I stared out the passenger window, remembering countless mornings driving Benji to school. Different car, different child, different life. But so achingly similar.

We pulled up to the school, and Benny leaned forward between the seats. "Bye Mom," he said to Deenie, then turned to me with a thoughtful look. "Bye Other Mom."

I managed a weak smile as he hopped out. We watched him join the stream of children flowing into the building.

"Ready?" Deenie asked softly.

I nodded, though I wasn't sure what exactly I was ready for. The DNA test? The answers? The truth about who we were and how we'd been separated?

"Ready," I echoed, and we pulled away from the curb, leaving Benny behind and driving toward whatever answers awaited us.

Chapter 27

Deenie and I entered the building of the police station, where Officers Rodriguez and Chen had already coordinated with Detective Lane to set up an appointment for our DNA test. We were taking a rapid test today along with a more comprehensive test which would provide official results in a few weeks. The more I got to know Deenie though, the more I knew we didn't need either of these tests. We were sisters.

The lab technician barely glanced at our matching faces as she swabbed our cheeks. "Results in about an hour," she said, labeling the samples.

We sat in a waiting room and a few moments later, a knock sounded, then the door opened. In walked Detective Lane. He glanced at me, then Deenie.

"I'm Deenie," she said, raising her hand.

His eyes crinkled with a smile before his expression returned to neutral. "Have you ladies been swabbed yet?"

We both nodded, and he sat across from us in one of the other two chairs that were in the tiny room.

We sat in the waiting room, all of us on pins and needles thought we already knew what the results would show. Every few minutes, Deenie's leg would bounce, and I'd catch myself doing the same thing.

"Ms. Price," Detective Lane said softly, turning to Deenie. "Did you take the day off work to be here?"

Their eyes met for a moment too long. A slight blush colored Deenie's cheeks as she shook her head. "No, actually - funny story. I work remotely for an online magazine, just like Nadine."

Detective Lane's eyes widened. He looked at me. "Seriously?"

Deenie's smile grew. "Yes," she answered. "I was telling Nadine earlier, last night I did a ton of research about twin studies. You would not believe the kinds of results they've found about identical twins who were reared apart."

Detective Lane cleared his throat. "I... uh... I did some research myself last night on the same thing."

Deenie gasped. "You did?"

I listened as Deenie chatted with Detective Lane like they were old friends. I had inadvertently stumbled upon one clear difference between us: Deenie was clearly an extrovert, while I was the more introverted twin.

When the technician reentered the room, my hands were trembling. She handed us each an envelope, but we already knew what they would say.

"99.9% match," Deenie whispered, staring at her results.

"Identical twins," I confirmed, the words feeling strange in my mouth.

Detective Lane cleared his throat, his tone all businesslike now. "The comprehensive test will tell us more, but this confirms what we suspected."

I looked at Deenie – my sister – and saw the same questions in her eyes. How? Why? Who had separated us?

But beneath those questions, a harder truth was crystallizing: Benny wasn't Benji. Benny was my nephew, a child who looked like my son because his mother and I shared the same DNA. The similarity that had drawn me here, that had given me such hope, was just a cruel coincidence.

"I'll make some calls," Detective Lane said, his hand brushing Deenie's arm. "Start looking into hospital records from '94."

The drive back to Deenie's house was quiet. She kept glancing at me, opening her mouth as if to speak, then closing it again.

Inside, I made it as far as the living room before the tears started. Deenie wrapped her arms around me, and I broke down completely.

"I'm sorry," she whispered. "I'm so sorry about Benji."

I pulled away, wiping my eyes. "I thought... when I saw Benny, I thought..."

"I know."

"I need to be alone." My voice cracked. "Please."

She nodded, understanding in her eyes – my eyes – as I retreated to the guest room and closed the door.

Sitting on the bed, I pulled out my phone and stared at the DNA results again. I had found a sister I never knew existed, but I was still no closer to finding my son.

The tears came harder now, and I buried my face in the pillow to muffle my sobs. Somewhere out there, Benji was still missing. And now I knew for certain that the boy I'd followed here wasn't him at all.

Chapter 28

I didn't know how I got through the night. Somehow, I was able to get through lunch and dinner with Deenie, her growing more and more excited the more we learned of each other, while I felt more and more empty.

I understood her position, of course. Meeting a long-lost sister who happened to be your twin? Every non-twin kid had to have dreamed of such a possibility at least once. But I couldn't fully share in her excitement because part of me was still missing.

Deenie had Benny, but where was Benji?

The next morning, my phone buzzed for the hundredth time. Tom's name flashed on the screen, and I finally answered, bracing myself for him to curse me out.

"Jesus, Nadine, what's going on? I've been calling you and texting you all day."

His words stung because I knew he was saying them out of hurt and frustration. But Tom couldn't possibly know how I was feeling right now. Neither could Clara or Angelique, but I owed them all a full explanation.

"Hold on," I said. "Let me add Clara and Angelique to the call."

A few clicks later, and their concerned voices filled my ear.

"Are you okay?" Angelique said.

"What do you mean, she looks exactly like you?" Clara chimed in.

"Start from the beginning!" Tom said.

I took a deep breath. "Remember when I said I thought I saw Benji at that school?" My voice wavered.

Silence filled their ends of the line, which let me know they were hanging on my every word.

I sighed. "Well, I did see a boy who looks exactly like him. Because... because his mother is my identical twin sister."

Silence.

"Your what?" Clara finally managed.

"I didn't know either," I clarified, though it was obvious because why would I keep something like this from my best friend if I had known it? "We just found out yesterday. The DNA test confirmed it." I swallowed hard. "Her name is Deenie. Nadeen, just like me, but she spells hers differently. She has a son named Benny who looks just like Benji because... because we're identical twins. Benny's name is also Benjamin, which was why I freaked out when I saw his name in the caption of the picture. And then..."

My eyes clouded as the reality of the situation hit me once again.

"Holy shit," Tom whispered.

"But your parents never said anything about a twin, right?" Angelique asked.

"No, they didn't," I said in a frustrated tone. Angelique's question had opened another wound. Why had my parents ever told me I had a twin sister? Had they given Deenie up at birth and chosen not to say anything? Why not keep both of us? Was I their real daughter? There were so many things I didn't understand. "That's the thing –" I continued, "Deenie says she wasn't adopted either. Her parents are still alive and never told her anything." I ran a hand through my hair. "None of it makes sense."

"Are you sure you're okay?" Clara asked softly. "This is... a lot."

"I'm not okay," I admitted. "But I need answers. And I need to find Benji. The real Benji."

After a few more minutes of questions I couldn't answer, I ended the call. The silence of the guest room pressed in around me.

I found myself standing outside Deenie's bedroom door. My knuckles hesitated against the wood before finally knocking.

"Come in," she called.

Deenie sat cross-legged on her bed, surrounded by old photo albums. She looked up at me with red-rimmed eyes that matched my own.

"I've been looking through all my baby pictures," she said. "There's nothing before I was three months old. Mom always said there was a fire at our old house, that's why..."

"Deenie," I interrupted softly. "We need to talk to your parents."

She nodded slowly. "I know. I've been sitting here trying to work up the courage to call them." She picked up her cell phone, then set it down again. "How do you even start that conversation? 'Hey Mom, Dad, funny story – remember when you never mentioned I had an identical twin sister?'"

"We deserve answers," I said, my voice stronger than I felt. "About who we are. About what happened to us."

Deenie looked at me for a long moment, then picked up her phone again. "You're right." She took a deep breath. "Let's find out the truth."

Chapter 29

All these recent events were weighing on me in ways I could not describe. It was too much for my brain to handle - I felt like I was having an out of body experience and the real me was just floating through this situation watching myself go through the motions as Deenie and I searched for answers about our birth and our true parentage.

The doorbell rang at exactly two o'clock. Deenie and I exchanged nervous glances.

"Maybe you should wait in the kitchen," she suggested. "Just... just for a minute. I'll tell them what happened and then we can introduce you to my parents."

I nodded and stepped out of sight, my heart hammering as I heard the door open.

"Mom, Dad," Deenie's voice carried through the house. "Thanks for coming."

"Of course, sweetheart," a woman's voice answered. "You sounded so strange on the phone. Is everything alright?"

"You might want to sit down first."

I heard the shuffle of movement, the creak of the living room furniture.

"Deenie, you're scaring us," a man's voice said. "What's going on?"

Deenie was silent for a moment, then she said. "Well... I recently found... there's something..." Her voice trailed off and after a few more moments I realized she probably didn't know where to begin.

Taking my cue, I stepped into the doorway.

The reaction was immediate. Her mother's hand flew to her mouth, her father half-rose from his seat, then fell back heavily.

"What..." her mother breathed. "How..."

"This is Nadine," Deenie said, her voice trembling slightly. "We met yesterday. We took a DNA test. We're identical twins."

The color drained from both their faces. Her father reached for her mother's hand.

"That's... that's not possible," her mother whispered, but the truth was written all over their faces.

"Isn't it?" Deenie's voice had an edge I hadn't heard before. "Because we have proof. What we don't have are answers."

The silence stretched until her father cleared his throat. "We should have told you long ago," he said quietly.

"Told me what?"

"That you were adopted." Her mother's voice cracked. "We wanted to tell you so many times, but..." She wiped at her eyes. "You were only three months old when you came to us. We loved you so much, and as time went on, it got harder and harder to find the right moment."

"Did you know?" I asked, speaking for the first time. "About me?"

They both shook their heads. "The adoption agency never mentioned a twin," her father said. "We only knew that your birth mother had surrendered her parental rights. They told us it was a closed adoption."

Deenie sank onto the couch, her legs seeming to give out. "All this time... Why didn't you tell me I was adopted?"

"We were afraid," her mother admitted. "Afraid you'd feel different, or that you'd want to find your birth parents instead of..." She trailed off, tears flowing freely now.

"I would never..." Deenie started, then stopped. She looked at me, then back at her parents. "You're my parents. Nothing changes that. But this..." She gestured between us. "We need to know the truth."

Her father nodded, pulling out his phone. "The agency was called New Horizons. They're still operating, I think." He typed something, then showed us the screen. "Here's their number. Maybe they can tell you more about what happened."

I stared at the numbers, feeling like they might hold the key to unlocking our past. But as I glanced at Deenie's shell-shocked expression and her parents' guilty faces, I wondered if we were ready for whatever truth we might find. I didn't know if it was paranoia talking, but our story already felt so bizarre to me.

"Thank you," I said softly, saving the number to my phone. It was a start, at least. A first step toward understanding how we'd been separated, and why.

Chapter 30

We had some of the answers about what happened with our birth, but there was still so much we didn't know. Were my parents Deenie's birth parents, or was I adopted too? If so, why only keep one twin and allow the other to be raised by a different family? The more I thought about it, the less it made sense. The possibility came to me that I was adopted too, but I didn't want to believe that. I had already suffered so many losses in my life - now I was about to lose the only parents I'd ever known too?

My parents were already deceased from a car crash a decade ago. Finding out I was adopted would be like losing them twice.

If my parents weren't my biological parents, who were me and Deenie's biological parents? Why did they give us up? Had they ever wondered about us? Tried to find us?

The next day while Benny was at school, Deenie and I traveled to New Horizons. We had called them yesterday after Deenie's parents explained their side of the story, so they were expecting us. The paperwork was supposed to be ready when we got there.

"Both adopted," I repeated, staring at the paperwork from New Horizons. "Separated at three months old."

Detective Lane faced us with a pained smile like he felt sorry for us finding out all these secrets during such a sensitive time. He had agreed to meet us here to aid in our investigation about our birth origin. It was nice of him to agree to help us though our situation had nothing to do with Benji's case. Maybe he was doing it out of pity for me.

"I'm afraid I have some... unfortunate news," he said, and I braced myself for what could be coming next.

"What is it?" Deenie asked, searching his eyes.

Detective Lane cleared his throat. "Your birth father... I was able to find information about him."

Deenie's eyes lit up. "You did?"

Detective Lane gave her a pained smile. "Yes, but... he died of an overdose."

Those words hit me like ice water down my back. If our birth father was dead, what about our birth mother? If she was dead too, we might never learn the full story.

As if sensing my question, Detective Lane leaned forward in his chair. "Let me make some calls. With both adoption records, we might be able to trace your birth mother."

Deenie and I shared a look before we silently agreed. It was weird how I had known her less than a week and already could read what she was thinking. It was as if we had known each other all our lives.

Sometime later, we pulled into my driveway so Deenie could officially meet my friends. Three familiar figures were already waiting on my porch.

"Here we go," I muttered to Deenie.

Clara spotted us first, elbowing Tom and Angelique. Their jaws dropped in perfect sync as we stepped out of the car.

"Holy..." Angelique breathed.

"...shit," Clara finished.

Tom just stared, his eyes moving between us like he was watching a tennis match.

His eyes settled on me and my heart fluttered with relief. I didn't know how he did it, but Tom was able to tell us apart. He approached us with his eyes trained on me.

"So," I said, tearing my gaze away from Tom to make the introductions, "this is Deenie. Deenie, meet my friends – Clara, Angelique, and Tom."

"This is absolutely wild," Clara declared, circling us. "It's like seeing double."

"At least now we know why Nadine always hated her reflection," Angelique joked. "She was just missing her other half."

I appreciated how my friends were keeping the situation lighthearted though this was hardly a laughing matter. Deenie seemed excited to meet my people and she was already chatting up a storm with Clara and Angelique.

I didn't mind it because I had already reached my psychological limit days ago. I welcomed not being the center of attention.

We moved inside, and I watched as my friends continued to absorb Deenie into their orbit. Clara grilled her about her online writing career while Angelique demanded to know if Deenie and I shared the same terrible taste in movies. It felt surreal, these two parts of my life colliding.

"This is intense," Tom said, joining me in the kitchen as I sat in silence. "You okay?"

I looked up at him, noticing how his concerned expression softened when our eyes met. "I don't know," I admitted. "Everything's happening so fast. Detective

Lane says he is going to find our birth mother. I don't know what I'm going to do if he does. Our birth father is dead. What if she's dead too?"

Tom stepped closer, his hand brushing mine as he reached for a coffee mug. "Whatever happens, you've got backup. All of us." His fingers lingered against mine for a moment longer than necessary.

"Thanks," I said softly, feeling warmth spread across my cheeks.

A burst of laughter from the living room broke the moment. Deenie was doing an impression of our shared mannerisms while Clara and Angelique howled with recognition.

"Oh God, she does that thing with her hands too!" Clara exclaimed.

"Nature versus nurture, right there," Angelique added.

Tom grinned. "Come on, let's rescue your sister before they start asking for embarrassing stories."

"Too late," Deenie called from the other room. "They already told me about the karaoke incident!"

"Traitors," I muttered, but I was smiling as Tom and I rejoined the group. I didn't know how he always had that effect on me. Tom could get me to smile during my darkest moments. That had to count for something, but I couldn't dwell on it now. Instead, I filed it in the back of my mind for later.

Watching my friends with Deenie, I felt something shift inside me. For the first time since finding her, it felt less like my life was being invaded and more like it was expanding. If Detective Lane was successful, we would face our birth mother and whatever truth she held. But tonight, in this room full of laughter and friendship, I could breathe a little easier.

Tom caught my eye again from across the room and winked. My heart did a little flip that had nothing to do with long-lost sisters or missing sons.

"So," Clara was saying to Deenie, "has Nadine told you about the time she tried to learn how to breakdance?"

"No!" I protested as Tom grinned.

I shot him a murderous glare. He was supposed to be on my side.

His grin widened and I rolled my eyes.

"Oh, now this I have to hear," Deenie said, settling in with a mischievous smile of her own.

Chapter 31

Traveling back and forth to Sawsucket was starting to feel like second nature. Barely a week had passed and Detective Lane called with the news that he had found our biological mother. When I called Deenie, she was excited, but I didn't know how to feel. How could she be so accepting of all this? It bothered me but then I remembered that although Deenie and I seemed to share everything else, the one thing we didn't share was a missing child. I would never wish this pain on my sister or anyone else for that matter. Our biological mother worked outside the home, so the only time she was free was on Saturdays. Deenie said she could make it but she had to bring Benny. I was cool with that, but I wasn't sure if it was a good idea.

"What if she's...?" I started to ask, before I realized I hadn't fully formulated my question. "What if things don't go well?" I finished after a few moments.

Deenie shrugged. "I figure things can't go that badly if she agreed to meet us."

She was probably right, but I was still leery of the whole situation.

Deenie and Benny rode in my car while I drove to the house in Chicopee, Massachusetts while Detective Lane followed us. Deenie had driven Benny to my house earlier in the day so we could all ride over together.

Benny was a chatterbox like his mom, so he and Deenie occupied each other while I tuned them out and focused on the road. Forty five minutes on the highway, and we were in Chicopee.

Deenie, Benny, and I stared while Detective Lane pulled up and parked on the street behind us. A red car was parked in the driveway.

The small house needed paint, and the yard was overgrown with mismatched lawn ornaments scattered everywhere.

We each stepped out of our vehicles and stared at each other before heading toward the front door, Benny and Deenie falling silent and Benny grasping Deenie's hand.

Detective Lane reached out and the doorbell chimed with an off-key melody.

"Coming, coming!" A singsong voice called from inside. The door swung open to reveal a thin woman in her fifties, wearing a bright floral dress and at least four different styles of necklaces.

She froze, her eyes going wide. "Oh," she breathed. "Oh my stars. My girls. My beautiful, beautiful girls."

Before either of us could react, she grabbed our hands, pulling us inside. "Come in, come in! I made cookies. I always make cookies on Tuesdays. Or is it Wednesday? The fairies sometimes mix up my days."

Deenie and I shared a bewildered look, but we followed Detective Lane inside.

The interior was cluttered with collections of everything imaginable – porcelain dolls, wind chimes hanging from the ceiling, stacks of newspapers, and dozens of half-finished craft projects.

"Ms. Sullivan," Detective Lane began gently. "We'd like to ask you some questions."

"Call me Lucy," she said, bouncing on her toes. "Or Mom. Can you call me Mom? Is that weird? You're both so pretty. Just like I imagined. Do you want cookies?" She bent down to face Benny. "How about you, cutie pie? God, he's so adorable!"

Straightening her stance, she clapped her hands and spun in a circle, ending in a curtsy. "I am so happy to greet my guests." Then she disappeared into the kitchen, still chattering.

"She's..." Deenie whispered.

"Not all there," I finished.

Lucy returned with a plate of burnt cookies. "I knew you'd find me one day. The stars told me you would. Or maybe it was the lady at the grocery store. She knows things."

"Ms. Sullivan," Lane tried again. "Do you remember why the twins were separated?"

Her face clouded. "Separated? No, no. I just couldn't keep them. The doctors said I wasn't... wasn't right to be a mother. But I loved them. Love them." She reached out to touch our faces, and I forced myself not to flinch. "They said they'd find them a good home. Both of them. Together."

We stared at each other for a few moments, none of us sure how to proceed with our questions. Lucy extended the cookies toward us. "Take one," she urged. "I baked them special, just for all of you."

The cookies were so black they were barely decipherable, but I politely took one, along with Deenie, Benny, and Detective Lane. I could tell none of us had the heart to turn Lucy down.

Once we each had our cookies, Lucy stared as if waiting for us to eat them. Then her eyes widened as she raised her fingers. "Wait... milk!"

She hurried to the kitchen, and Detective Lane moved quickly. "Here," he gestured, reaching for each of our cookies. We handed them over and he stuffed them into his pockets.

Lucy returned five minutes later with no milk. She was wringing her hands with an apologetic look in her eyes. "So sorry dears, I ran out of milk."

"It's okay," Deenie said, stepping forward and taking over the conversation. "The cookies were delicious, thank you... Mom."

The word sounded foreign on her lips and I cringed when she said it, but Lucy's eyes lit up like a Christmas tree.

"You're quite welcome! Come, sit!"

Lucy led us to her haphazard looking couch and we all sat politely, then she began to tell us all about her life.

It turned out, she was a very interesting woman and I could tell that she was where Deenie got her extroverted personality.

We left thirty minutes later with more questions than answers.

Back at the adoption agency, Benny sat in the waiting room playing on his tablet while Deenie and I met with the director.

"Ah," the elderly woman said, reviewing some old files that were discovered after the ones that were already shown to us. "Yes, now I remember this case. It was... complicated."

She explained how our birth mother had been deemed unfit due to mental illness. How my parents had initially planned to adopt both of us.

"But you developed an infection, Deenie," she said. "You were in the hospital for weeks. The Wilson's couldn't wait – they were afraid of losing their chance at adoption entirely, so they took Nadine. By the time you recovered, another family had applied to adopt you."

"And no one thought to mention we had a twin?" I demanded.

The director looked uncomfortable. "It was a different time. The philosophy then was clean breaks, fresh starts. We... we didn't always prioritize keeping siblings together."

My heart couldn't sink any further. The more we learned about our past and how we were adopted, the less I wanted to know anymore. I wanted all of this to go away. I wanted to go to sleep and wake up with Benji in my arms, and laugh about how this had all been a tragic nightmare.

But I wasn't asleep so I couldn't be dreaming. All of this was very real.

Later that evening, back at my house, Benny insisted on making us his "special" hot chocolate – mostly Swiss Miss with an obscene amount of marshmallows.

"So you're my for-real aunt?" he asked me, chocolate mustache on his upper lip.

"Looks like it," I said.

"Cool. Does that mean I get double birthday presents?"

Deenie snorted into her mug while I laughed – really laughed – for the first time in days.

"You know what we should do?" Deenie said suddenly. "Take identical twin pictures. Really lean into the creepy factor."

"Make everyone do double takes?" I grinned.

"Exactly."

"Can I be in them too?" Benny asked.

"Of course, buddy," I said. "You can be our evil mastermind."

We spent the next hour taking increasingly ridiculous photos, with Benny directing us like a tiny Hollywood producer. By the time we collapsed on the couch, my sides hurt from laughing.

"This doesn't fix everything," Deenie said softly.

"No," I agreed, thinking of Benji. "But it's something good in the middle of all this crazy."

"We'll find him," she promised, squeezing my hand. "All three of us will look."

Benny, half-asleep between us, nodded solemnly. "Four of us. I'm good at finding things. Last week I found Mom's car keys in the freezer."

"That was one time," Deenie protested, but she was smiling.

I looked at my sister – my twin – and my nephew, feeling a strange mix of loss and discovery. We had so much more to figure out, but at least we wouldn't be doing it alone anymore.

Chapter 32

Now that the excitement of taking silly photos had died down, I was back to my depressing thoughts. It was strangely comfortable to have my twin and my nephew here with me, but my heart longed for Benji.

Would I ever find him?

Would I ever see my baby again?

I sat on the couch as Deenie and Benny chattered away, Benny fighting to keep his eyes open but forcing himself to stay awake because he was excited about his newfound auntie. I couldn't help but to fall in love with the little boy. He reminded me so much of Benji that it hurt.

After another hour, Deenie and Benny's chatter died down and Benny fell asleep. Deenie carried him to the loveseat and I covered him with a blanket while she propped a pillow under his head.

"There," she said, then grinned at me. "Teamwork makes the dream work, right?"

I forced a smile.

"What's wrong?" she asked, but I shook my head. Though she was extraordinarily caring throughout this ordeal, I didn't want to unload my pain onto my sister.

We sat back on the couch, both lost in our thoughts. The weight of our lost years hung heavy between us.

"All this time," Deenie whispered. "We could have grown up together. Been there for each other."

"Had actual twin adventures instead of taking fake twin photos thirty years too late," I added, trying to smile.

Deenie hesitated, then asked, "What about Benji's father? Has he been helping with the search?"

I studied her. I could tell that she was asking out of genuine concern, but also because she was curious. I was curious about her too. She wasn't wearing a wedding ring and I'd never seen her mention Benny's father either.

My throat tightened. "No, he... he's dead. They both are."

"Both?" Deenie seemed confused.

I took a deep breath. "Roman was my first love. High school sweethearts. We were always breaking up and getting back together over stupid things. During one of our 'off' periods, I met Gino." My hands started trembling. "He was charming at first. Then controlling. Then violent."

Deenie reached for my hand.

"Roman helped me get away from Gino," I continued. "He'd always been my safe place, you know? But Gino..." I swallowed hard. "He followed me to my old apartment. Roman was in the middle of helping me move. Everything was restored between us. We had finally gotten ourselves on the right track for the sake of our son. But Gino came while we were loading up the truck and he had a gun..."

"Oh, Nadine," Deenie said as she imagined how the rest of the story went.

"Gino went to prison. Died there a couple months ago, right after Benji was taken." I wiped my eyes. "Sometimes I think if Roman and I had just stayed together, if we hadn't been so young and stupid about everything..."

"Hey," Deenie said softly. "It wasn't your fault."

I fell silent as I reminisced about Roman and how in love we were. Our relationship wasn't perfect, of course, but I knew in my heart that that last time, we were going to finally settle our differences. We had both matured over the years and if life had given us another chance, we would still be together. Still lost in thought, I barely registered Deenie's next words.

"God, this is going to sound crazy, but I actually understand everything you just told me," she started. "Benny's father... he was abusive too. That's why we moved to Connecticut from Massachusetts. I never told him where we went. Just disappeared one night."

Something tickled at the back of my mind. "Massachusetts?" I repeated. "You lived in Massachusetts?"

Deenie nodded.

"Where?"

"Millbrook. It's near—"

"Ashland," I finished. My heart started racing. "Deenie, when exactly did you leave?"

She looked puzzled. "About a year ago. Why?"

"I need..." My mouth went dry. "Can I see a picture of him? Of Benny's father?"

"I guess, but I don't understand—"

"Please."

Frowning, she pulled out her phone and scrolled through her photos. "I only kept this one so I'd recognize him if he ever showed up." She turned the screen toward me.

The world tilted sideways.

"Oh my God," I whispered.

Chapter 33

Within seconds, I was up on my feet and my fingers were scrambling to dial Detective Lane's name.

Deenie stood next to me, looking just as shell-shocked as I felt.

"Hello?" he answered in a groggy tone.

Deenie and I both started rambling at once.

"One at a time," Detective Lane said, sounding like he was still gathering his bearings. "What are you two trying to tell me?"

"Show him," I urged Deenie.

She pulled up the photo of her ex, Adrian, on her phone, then texted it to me and I forwarded it to Detective Lane.

A few moments later, he said, "Okay, I got it. Now what's going on?"

"That's Benny's father," Deenie explained. "Adrian Mitchell. I left him a year ago. Benny and I fled from Massachusetts to Connecticut."

"And look at this," I added, pulling up an old photo of Roman, Benji's father, and sending that to Detective Lane too. "This is Benji's father, Roman."

We waited with baited breath for Detective Lane to put two and two together like we had just done.

Detective Lane spoke slowly as he compared the two men. "Similar build, similar features..."

"But different men," I finished. "The major difference is that Adrian wears a beard, while Roman was always clean shaven."

Detective Lane fell silent and my mind grew wild as I waited for him to catch up to what we were trying to tell him. Finally, I couldn't take it anymore. I let it all out, no longer caring if he didn't believe my theory. I had to find out if it was true.

"Detective, remember how I told you Benji said his daddy bought him ice cream that day?"

"Yes...?" was his tentative reply.

I continued with a sigh. "Benji kept saying he saw his daddy in the weeks before he disappeared. He said his daddy bought him ice cream the day he was taken."

"Yes, but the surveillance footage never showed—"

"Because the cameras never showed his face, right?" Deenie interrupted. "You guys saw the red jacket and the hat he was wearing, but the images would have never picked up Adrian's face."

My next words tumbled out of my mouth, my entire body trembling with nerves as I spoke them. "Benji was only four when Roman died. He was in therapy, struggling to process it. The therapist said he might have issues with loss and abandonment..."

"So when Benji saw someone who looked like Roman..." Detective Lane began, as if he was finally catching up with the story.

"He thought it was his father," I finished, my voice cracking. "All this time, I thought he was just having trouble accepting that Roman was gone. But what if he really did see someone? What if he saw Adrian?"

"And Adrian," Deenie added, her face pale, "would have seen a little boy who looked exactly like his own son. The son who I took away from him, to get away from his abuse."

Detective Lane fell silent once again.

My mind scrambled like it was on the brink of solving a nearly impossible mathematical equation.

His voice came back on the line. "You think Adrian took Benji because he looked like Benny?"

My heart pricked at his words because it didn't seem like he believed it. "It makes sense," I insisted. "Deenie left him, took his son. They lived in Massachusetts, just like me and Benji, but he didn't know they moved to Connecticut. He was angry, probably looking for them. Then he sees a little boy who could be Benny's twin in a different city..."

"And he probably thought I was hiding in plain sight," Deenie whispered. "Using a different last name, pretending to be someone else."

"The ice cream, the approaching him slowly, gaining his trust..." Lane muttered, as if the pieces were falling into place for him. "A child that age, seeing someone who looked so much like his dead father..."

"He would have gone with him willingly," I said, feeling sick. "Benji would have thought his daddy had come back."

A fleeting memory of me being struck in the back of my head came back to me, but I squelched it. Benji wouldn't have gone willingly in that situation, or at least, I didn't think so, but if Adrian told him a convincing enough story...

Lane's voice filled the line again. "I'm putting out an APB on Adrian Mitchell. We'll need all the information you have − known associates, previous addresses, any places he might go."

"He has a brother in Vermont," Deenie said. "And an old cabin in the Berkshires that his parents gifted him. He used to take Benny there for fishing trips."

"Write everything down," Lane instructed, sounding like he was moving around frantically wherever he was. "Every detail you can remember. I'll be there within the hour."

As Deenie began writing frantically using a pen and notepad I eagerly supplied her, Lane continued. "We're going to find him, Nadine. This is the break we've been waiting for."

I nodded, unable to speak. My heart pitter-pattered with anticipation because the worry I felt about Detective Lane not believing our story dissipated.

He did believe me, and now we were going to find Benji.

Seventy-six days of waiting, imagining the worst, and now we might finally have an answer. But knowing that my son had been lured away by someone he thought was his father – it made my heart break all over again.

Deenie reached for my hand. "We're close," she whispered. "I can feel it."

I squeezed her hand back, my mind on Detective Lane and hoping he was assembling his team right now like he said he was. I had half a mind to snatch the papers that Deenie was writing on and rush off to the locations myself to find my son.

After all this time, all the dead ends and false hopes, we finally had a real lead. My mind and heart were both screaming that the mystery had been solved. Somewhere out there, Adrian Mitchell had my son. And now we were going to find him.

Chapter 34

Detective Lane crouched behind his vehicle, checking his weapon for the third time. Ten years on missing persons, and nights like these never got easier. Especially not with Nadine Wilson's face haunting him, her hope both inspiring and terrifying. She'd already lost so much - finding a twin sister and nephew only to lose her son would be beyond cruel. "Not tonight," he whispered, holstering his gun. "Tonight, we bring him home."

The crew already had a plan. They would start with the cabin in the Berkshires rather than heading to Vermont. Hopefully the boy was in the cabin so they could finally lay this case to rest.

Six squad cars were parked outside the cabin. From the looks of it, someone was inside. The lights were on, which was a good sign. Through binoculars, Detective Lane studied each window. At one of the back windows, he had clear sight of what looked to be Adrian Mitchell. After looking at the photo on his phone, then through his binoculars, he confirmed that he was correct.

"The suspect is in sight," he said into his walkie talkie.

A few moments later, "Copy," a voice said through the speakers. "What about the boy?"

Detective Lane held up his binoculars again. He scanned the room, which was difficult to do from his angle. From the looks of it, Adrian was sitting on the couch, but after craning his neck to see, Benji wasn't present.

His heart sank.

He spoke into the walkie talkie. "No sight of the... wait!" A glimmer of movement passed, and Detective Lane's eyes were back in his binoculars again. "I see the boy!" Adrenaline coursed his veins once again. "He's sitting next to the suspect on the couch."

"Any signs of injury?"

Detective Lane studied Benji, who had just come from another room – probably the bathroom – to join Adrian. "Not that I can see."

"Copy. Let us know when you're ready to move."

Detective Lane's defenses were on high alert. The boy was in sight and he appeared to be unharmed. If Adrian Mitchell cooperated, this could be an easy transition. There was no way for the man to get out of this. The cabin was surrounded and Detective Lane would be damned before he let that man escape with Benjamin Wilson. Not when the boy was merely feet away.

Still, he knew these situations could go left easily, so he proceeded with caution.

Slowly emerging from behind his vehicle, he crept toward the cabin.

Adrian and Benji were still sitting in front of the TV, seemingly oblivious to the tension outside the cabin.

Detective Lane spoke into his walkie talkie again. "All clear. Approach quietly, gentlemen. Let's make this a smooth transition tonight."

"Copy," came a voice from the other end, and slowly, the rest of the crew mirrored his actions, emerging from their vehicles and quietly closing their doors.

Until the last set of officer's doors closed with a loud creaking sound that jerked Adrian from his seat.

"Shit!" Detective Lane said, ducking so he would be out of sight, but not before Adrian's head whipped toward the window and he was seen.

"Fuck!"

Detective Lane hid behind a nearby tree as the other officers ducked for cover too. It was no use, however, because all Adrian had to do was look outside and he would see their squad cars outside his cabin.

Detective Lane peeked out after a few moments with no activity and saw that Adrian was standing near the window. He opened it wide and shouted outside.

"Who's that out there! Show yourself!"

Detective Lane caught eyes with one of the crew members and gave him a signal. The crew member nodded, then signaled to the other members to surround the cabin on all sides.

"I said, show yourself!" Adrian yelled.

Once Detective Lane received the nod, he moved from around the tree and stepped forward, holding his hands up. "Adrian Mitchell, I'm Detective Lane. Can you step outside so we can have a conversation?"

Adrian's features became filled with suspicion.

"Hell no, I ain't stepping outside! What's this about? Why are you here?"

Detective Lane forced an even tone. "I think you know why I'm here, Mr. Mitchell." He slowly took a step forward and Adrian tensed, so he stopped moving.

"Stay back!" Adrian warned.

"Okay," Detective Lane said, his arms still up in a non-threatening stance, but he tried to peek and see if the boy was still on the couch. He was, and from the frightened look on his face, Detective Lane sensed that he didn't know what was going on.

"Mr. Mitchell," he began again. "As I said before, I just want to have a conversation."

"A conversation about what?" A sarcastic smirk filled Adrian's features.

Detective Lane took another step forward and he saw movement behind Adrian. One of the other officers had somehow gotten inside the cabin – likely an unlocked door or window, since Adrian would undoubtedly have heard a window breaking or door being bashed in.

The officer nodded, then crept toward the boy, but the boy screamed, "Daddy!" and all hell broke loose.

Adrian turned, and that was when Detective Lane saw him whip the gun from his waistband, pointing it at the officer.

"Drop the weapon!" Detective Lane and the officer yelled in unison.

"I ain't dropping shit!" Adrian screamed. "Ain't none of you sorry bastards about to take my boy!"

"He's not your son!" Detective Lane yelled, hoping he could get through to Adrian and still reach an amicable solution.

Adrian's sarcastic reply was immediate. "The hell he ain't! I had the DNA test done the day he was born. He's my boy!"

"No, he's not! That's what I'm trying to explain to you," Detective Lane said, inching closer and closer as the other officers who were outside the cabin did the same.

"Clear shot on target," came the whispered voice in Detective Lane's walkie talkie, but he didn't dare answer.

"Get the fuck away from my cabin before I start shooting!" Adrian thundered, while Benji was visibly shaken. He was standing between the officer and his father.

"Mr. Mitchell, that won't be necessary," Detective Lane said in an even tone. "How about you drop the weapon and we sort this out together?"

"Ain't shit to sort out," Adrian said, his tone full of menace. "Like I already said, you ain't taking my boy."

Detective Lane contemplated the options. Adrian wasn't cooperating, which meant they might need to call for more backup.

He opened his mouth to say something else, when Adrian suddenly yelled, "You stop that right now!"

Detective Lane's eyes shot to the other officer, who appeared to have startled Adrian by his sudden movement.

Adrian trained his gun on the officer but whipped out another one and pointed it at the boy.

"No!" Detective Lane swore under his breath. "Mr. Mitchell..." he called out, but Adrian cut him off.

"You want my boy, it's gonna have to be in a body bag. That bitch will never get him back, as long as I live."

"Daddy!" Benji whimpered, and Detective Lane's heart broke at the sight.

"Mr. Mitchell, I..." He started, but before he could finish, a gunshot rang out, then pure pandemonium ensued.

"Benji!" Detective Lane screamed.

Chapter 35

Detective Lane had come and gone, saying the team was ready to go find Adrian. As soon as he left, I frantically called Tom, Clara, and Angelique. Each of them answered their phones sounding tired, but bounded out of their beds when I told them we might have finally found Benji.

Now everyone was piled into my house - Tom, Clara and Peter, Angelique, Deenie, and Benny, who had miraculously slept through all the excitement up to this point.

When Tom had walked in the door, I fell apart in his arms. He held me like he always did and assured me that everything would be okay.

"They're gonna find him, Nadine," he insisted. "It's only a matter of time."

Hours ticked by like years. Every phone buzz made us jump. Every car passing the house had us rushing to the windows.

Benny finally woke up, and Peter did a double take until Clara carefully explained that he was not Benji, but his cousin, Benny.

Peter, being a child, asked a few questions but eagerly accepted the news now that he had "double-godbrothers" - a term that he coined on the spot - and now he and Benny played video games on their tablets, oblivious to the rising tension amongst the adults. Clara stress-baked three batches of cookies. Angelique paced. Tom kept his hand on my shoulder, a steady anchor as my world spun on its axis.

"They'll find him," Deenie kept saying. "They have to."

I prayed they were right.

But as the morning fell with no word, and Peter and Benny laid out on the floor next to each underneath a shared blanket, my hope began to crumble.

"What if we're wrong?" I whispered to Tom. "What if Adrian doesn't have him? What if—"

"Don't," Tom said softly. "Don't go there."

But I was already spiraling. My chest tightened, each breath shorter than the last. The room started to spin.

"Nadine?" Tom's voice seemed far away. "Nadine, look at me. Breathe with me."

"I can't—" The walls were closing in. "I can't do this again. I can't—"

Clara appeared with a glass of water. Angelique grabbed my hand. Deenie knelt in front of me, coaching my breathing.

That was when we heard it. A knock at the door.

The room froze.

Tom squeezed my shoulder before rushing to answer it. I couldn't breathe, couldn't move, couldn't think.

The door opened.

Detective Lane stepped in, but he was alone.

My world crumbled. "No..." I groaned. "No... please!"

Detective Lane moved out of the way, and that was when I saw him.

"Benji!"

I screamed his name at the top of my lungs, startling and waking Peter and Benny at the same time.

My legs gave out as I ran to my baby. He crashed into my arms, solid and real and alive. His hair was longer, his face thinner, but his arms wrapped around my neck just like they used to.

"Mommy," he sobbed. "Mommy, I'm sorry. I thought... I thought he was Daddy."

"Shh, baby," I cried, holding him tighter. "It's okay. You're home now. You're safe."

Everyone was crying. Even Detective Lane had a tear in his eyes, though he cleared his throat and returned to a neutral tone as he explained that he had already brought Benji to the hospital to be cleared for injuries before bringing him home. He didn't want any further delays in me seeing my son.

"Thank you," I let out, my voice barely above a whisper as I repeatedly kissed the top of my son's head. "Thank you so much."

Benny was practically speechless as he continued staring wide-eyed at his newfound cousin. Deenie had her arms around both of us.

Tom was wiping his eyes, trying to pretend he wasn't.

"Where..." I looked up at Detective Lane again through my tears.

"The cabin," he confirmed. "Just like Deenie said. Adrian's in custody."

Benji pulled back slightly, his eyes finding Benny. They stared at each other with mirror expressions of confusion.

"Benji," I said softly, "there's someone I want you to meet. This is your cousin, Benny. And this is your Aunt Deenie."

"Cousin?" Benji's eyes went wide. "Like... for real?"

"For real," Benny confirmed, stepping closer. "Want to play Mario Kart? I'm really good."

"I'm better," Benji said automatically, then looked at me uncertainly.

I laughed through my tears. "Go ahead play, baby." Then I turned to Tom. "Can you set up his game in here? I don't want to ever let him out of my sight again."

Tom nodded and rushed to Benji's room to grab the game.

I watched the boys tumble onto the floor next to Peter, who was already inching up to the TV. Though my son was sitting right in front of me, I couldn't believe it. All that waiting, all that hoping and praying, and Benji was home.

The boys began arguing about who got to be Luigi.

Tom set up the TV, then his arm slipped around my waist as my legs threatened to give out again.

"He's really home," I whispered.

"He's really home," Tom confirmed, pressing a kiss to my temple.

Clara was already heading to the kitchen, mumbling about grabbing Benji some of his favorite cookies which she had baked in anticipation of his arrival.

Angelique was on the phone, presumably spreading the news with her Pastor. Her church had been praying for us every day.

Detective Lane was quietly explaining details about Adrian to Deenie.

Once the boys were deeply focused on their game, Deenie and Detective Lane walked toward me.

"I want to share with you what happened at the cabin," he said, but I held a hand up.

171

"I can't," I said, my brain finally catching up to the moment at hand and exhaustion threatening to make me collapse at any moment. My eyes blurred with tears. "I can't right now. Tomorrow."

Detective Lane nodded and after a few more moments of chatting with Deenie while Tom ushered me to the couch, he was gone.

Tom, Angelique, Deenie and Clara were all holding conversations around me, but all I could focus on was the sight and sound of my son's laughter mixing with his god brother and cousin. After almost three months of silence, it was the most beautiful sound I'd ever heard.

"We have so much to figure out," I said, once I snapped out of my stupor.

"Tomorrow," Tom said firmly. "Today, just be here. He's home."

Home. My son was home. And somehow, in the midst of this nightmare, I'd found not just him, but a whole family I never knew I had.

I continued to stare at the boys in awe, until suddenly, a playful squabble broke out among them. Benji exclaimed, "No fair! Mom, Benny's cheating!"

"Am not!"

"Are too!"

Peter laughed at the top of his lungs.

I laughed through fresh tears. Moments like these were priceless.

Epilogue

The investigation revealed a twisted path of near-misses and ironies. Adrian had been watching me for months, convinced I was Deenie living under an alias. He'd approached Benji at school and the park, building trust slowly.

The first time Adrian approached Benji, Benji said he couldn't be his daddy because his daddy was dead.

Adrian was furious because he thought Deenie had told his son that. He had no clue about Deenie having a twin sister or that Benji was not his son.

After some time, he convinced Benji that he was his father but to keep it a secret so Mommy wouldn't be upset.

My son, still wrestling with losing Roman, saw what he desperately wanted to see – his father coming back to him, so he agreed.

When the police found Adrian's hideout, they discovered fake passports and plane tickets to Argentina. We'd found Benji just days before Adrian planned to disappear with him forever, never realizing he had the wrong child, the wrong woman.

All while Deenie, the actual object of his obsession, lived just one town over.

Adrian's cabin in Massachusetts was only a few miles from the city line of Sawsucket, Connecticut.

When I heard about the brief shootout that occurred that ended with Adrian being shot in the chest, but surviving, I almost fainted from the possibility. Deenie was distraught as well, because if the shoe was on the other foot and it was Benny in that cabin, her son could have been shot and killed. Thankfully, Benji wasn't shot during the incident, though Detective Lane originally wasn't aware of who had opened fire.

***

Six months passed by like a blur, and life had found a new normal.

Benji still had nightmares, but his therapist said he was making remarkable progress. I had my own weekly sessions, learning to manage the anxiety that still gripped me whenever Benji was out of sight.

The boys – Benji, Benny, and Peter – were inseparable, trading off weekends between our houses. Clara joked that she had accidentally adopted two more sons.

Tonight, I was curled up on my couch, giggling with Deenie on FaceTime like we were teenagers making up for lost time.

"I have a secret," I said, biting my lip.

"No way, I have one too!" Deenie bounced on her screen. "You go first."

"Well..." I felt my cheeks warm. "Tom and I are officially together."

"Finally!" Deenie squealed. "But how dare you get a man at the same time as me?"

"Wait, what? Who's your man?"

"Michael," she said, grinning like a schoolgirl.

I scrunched my face. "Michael? Who the hell is that?"

Deenie burst into another fit of giggles. "Oh, my bad, sis. I know him as Michael, but you know him as Detective Lane."

My jaw dropped. "No way! Detective Lane? Our Detective Lane?"

"The very same," she said dreamily. "Turns out he's been calling me for 'follow-up questions' just to hear my voice."

I shook my head, laughing. "Our lives are ridiculous, you know that?"

"Says the woman who found her long-lost twin because their sons are identical."

We fell into comfortable silence, just smiling at each other through our screens.

"Hey Nadine?"

"Yeah?"

"I'm really glad we found each other."

"Me too," I said softly. "Even if it took us thirty years and a crazy series of events to get here."

From somewhere in her house, I heard Benny yell, "Mom! Benji's on the phone. Can he sleep over Friday?"

"Speaking of a crazy series of events," Deenie chuckled.

"You know what's really crazy?" I said. "All those years I spent looking in mirrors, hating my reflection... I was just missing my other half."

"Well, you're stuck with me now, sis."

"Wouldn't have it any other way."

Life had taken us down separate paths, through darkness and pain, only to bring us back together in the most unexpected way. But maybe that was how it was always meant to be – two mirrors finally facing each other, reflecting back all the pieces we didn't know were missing.

I hope you enjoyed *Long Way Home*. This story was a long time coming, but I hope you enjoyed reading it as much as I enjoyed piecing it together. What are your thoughts? I would love to hear from you. Share them in your review!

Want to read another thriller? Check out The Deadbeat from **The Red Series**. Nadine and Deenie's story was somewhat sweet and sentimental despite their circumstances of meeting each other, but Jessie and Belle are a whole different story...

Until next time,

Tanisha Stewart

Before you go...

If you enjoyed *Long Way Home*, I would absolutely love to hear your feedback. Please leave a **rating** or **review** commenting on your overall thoughts.

In addition, if you would like access to exclusive updates, giveaways, and more, join my email list at tanishastewartauthor.com/contact.

God bless you, and happy reading!

Tanisha Stewart

PS: If you would like to connect with me on social media, here's where you can find me:

Facebook: Tanisha Stewart, Author

Facebook group: Tanisha Stewart Readers
Instagram: tanishastewart_author
TikTok: authortanishastewart
Twitter: TStewart_Author
YouTube: Tanisha Stewart

The Deadbeat: A Psychological Thriller

A dangerous decision yanks two sisters out of the frying pan and lands them into the fire in this pulse pounding psychological thriller by the bestselling author of *Everybody Ain't Your Friend* and *The Quiet Ones* series.

After losing their beloved mother to ovarian cancer, identical twin sisters Jessie and Belle Brown's world is shattered to pieces. Their mother poured out her soul to help others, but in her time of need, the only ones who pitched in were strangers. Their deadbeat father refused to lift a finger in their direction.

Seething with rage over their father's absence, coupled with pain and agony over their mother's passing, the sisters need a place to channel their pain. Their selfish father seems to be the perfect target.

Will their plan to make him pay for his abandonment end in success? Or will it spark the beginning to the end of Jessie and Belle's ruin?

A pulse-pounding drama full of twists and turns. This series starter is fast-paced, straight to the point, and packs a powerful punch that will keep you on the edge of your seat.

The Red Series **is composed of self-contained stories – they can be read in any order.**

Check it out here: The Deadbeat: A Psychological Thriller

Every Voice Ain't From God: A Christian Romance Thriller

A psychological thriller with jaw-dropping twists and turns, and characters whose antics will leave you speechless... A story about love gone right, then wrong.

Zakari has known Nicole was **the one** since high school. He prays about whether their relationship is meant to be and receives confirmation one night during a church service. Zakari and Nicole are getting married!

Until **she breaks up with him** the next day.

Zakari plunges into a pit of despair, then Nicole reaches out and tells him they can be friends, maybe rekindle their relationship after college? Elated, Zakari agrees and bides his time until **he and Nicole can be together** again.

But Nicole gets **engaged to another man**, and Zakari doesn't understand.

He and Nicole are meant to be - she just needs to see it.

And **her fiancé needs to be eliminated**.

Every Voice Ain't From God is a twisted and page-turning tale about a man who will stop at nothing to have his woman's heart. **Including murder.**

Check it out here: <u>Every Voice Ain't From God: A Christian Romance Thriller</u>

Messed With The Wrong One: An Urban Romance Thriller

We all do things we live to regret, but when you harm the wrong ones, you get what you get.

Junior cheated. Marlena is furious. She resolves to teach him a lesson. What starts as a simple act of revenge, however, quickly takes a dangerous turn.

While Marlena was busy getting back at Junior, someone else happened to be planning a revenge of her own against Marlena. The deadly kind.

Marlena finds herself in a race against time to no longer change her man. Now she has to save him. And herself.

Check it out here: Messed With The Wrong One: An Urban Romance Thriller

Wrath (The 7 Deadly Sins Series)

Tony is a man after God's own heart. Saved from a past that was riddled with criminal activity, it is now his life's goal to build a future as a minister-in-training. With his beautiful wife, Meka, and their unborn child by his side, Tony feels life is complete.

Until he delivers his trial sermon, and tragedy strikes in the worst way.

Devastated by the blow he is dealt, Tony strives to shake it off and hold himself together. Tony clings onto hope, and things start to get better...until they get worse.

Dazed and confused with competing voices drowning his focus, Tony finds himself at his wits end. The Bible says that vengeance belongs to the Lord, but whose voice will Tony bow to - the Holy Spirit, or the venomous whispers of his flesh?

Check it out here: Wrath (The 7 Deadly Sins)

The Governor's Wife

He was sent to do **one job**.

Get rid of the man the Governor's wife was sleeping with.
A **single shot** was fired, and the mission should have been accomplished.

Instead, he shot the wrong person.

And now there's a **bounty on his head**.

The Governor's Wife is a fast-paced action thriller about a man who had one mission, but failed, and unbeknownst to him, that failed mission would unfold a whirlwind of conspiracies, secrets, and lies.

Check it out here: The Governor's Wife

Everybody Ain't Your Friend: An Urban Romance Thriller

They say you should keep your friends close, and enemies closer, but sometimes reality might be the other way around...

Mia thinks her life is completely normal. She has a loving boyfriend, great and supportive friends, and a close relationship with her mother.

Things take an interesting turn, however, when she is almost run down by a car one day. Then come the messages from an untraceable number. Not to mention the heartbreaking secret that is revealed shortly thereafter.

Suddenly, everything that Mia thought was right in her life goes wrong. She has no idea why, but she needs to find out, before her secret stalker decides her time is up.

Check it out here: <u>Everybody Ain't Your Friend: An Urban Romance Thriller</u>

Should Have Thought Twice: A Psychological Thriller

They say to always watch the quiet ones, because you never know when they might snap.

Shatina is a young woman with a troubled past and present. She lives in the shadows of her fraternal twin sister, who sucked up all the beauty genes, her best friend, whose seductive charm will sway any boy who listens, and her cousin, who is more than a knockout, but a force to be reckoned with.

Shatina feels like she has nothing going for her but her grades and her full scholarship to a four year institution of her choice... until someone comes along to threaten that.

Shatina has faced threats before, and little does anyone know, she has gained vindication over all of her enemies, one by one. Except this last one might be a bit more of a challenge than she bargained for.

Check it out here: <u>Should Have Thought Twice: A Psychological Thriller</u>

Not What It Seems: A Christian Romance Thriller

Sparks begin to fly between Priscilla and Raheem, but soon they will learn, all is not what it seems.

Priscilla moves across the country to escape a toxic ex who won't let her go. Her mindset is healing, but within days of her arrival, she's introduced to the sexiest man she's ever laid eyes on: **Raheem.**

When Priscilla and Raheem's eyes meet, the chemistry is immediate. One would think they are a match made in heaven, and everything will go smoothly for them.

Wrong.

Because the closer Priscilla and Raheem get to one another, the more strange things begin to happen.

Sinister things.

What has Priscilla gotten herself into?

She's locked into Raheem, and he wants her to stay, but as the song goes, **jealousy is cruel as the grave...** (*Song of Solomon 8:6*).

Check it out here: Not What It Seems: A Christian Romance Thriller

Clean Up Woman

What happens when dreams turn deadly?

Yana is a **workaholic**. She has noble aspirations but isn't taking care of home. Meanwhile, **Sasha**, her new **nanny**, is more than ready to step in. Sasha and **Yana's husband**, Shawn, get closer, arousing suspicion by Yana.

But there's more to this nanny than meets the eye. More than what Yana bargained for.

Clean Up Woman is a **gripping suspense thriller** with jaw-dropping **twists and turns** you won't see coming.

Check it out here: Clean Up Woman

Caught Up With The 'Rona: An Urban Sci Fi Thriller

Cordell's luck could not be any worse. A young black man, a full-time student, doing his best to give back to his community by serving as a substitute teacher, only to receive an email which stated that his job would be suspended for the next three weeks due to the Coronavirus.

Frustrated about the situation, he vents to his lifelong friend, Jerone. Shortly after their conversation begins, they are approached by Markellis, a neighborhood hustler who always tries to sell Cordell and Jerone on his get-rich-quick schemes...

But this one is different. Cordell is pressed for cash, so he convinces Jerone to go along with Markellis' proposal.

No sooner than they say yes, Cordell and Jerone are swept up in an almost unspeakable conspiracy, with less than three weeks to turn it around...

Only it's much more than just Cordell and Jerone's lives that are at stake.

Check it out here: Caught Up With The 'Rona: An Urban Sci Fi Thriller

December 21st: An Urban Supernatural Suspense

Flick is a regular guy, living a regular life, then the night of Thanksgiving came.

It all started with a conversation he had with his cousin Bru that got a little heated.

Tensions rose, but things calmed down when he went to his mother's house for the family dinner.

Little did he know, that's when his life would begin to shift in a direction that he never expected.

December 21st, Saturn and Jupiter aligning, competing belief systems... what did it all mean?
Nothing, Flick thought.
Until the first event.
Then the second.

Follow Flick's journey in this Urban Supernatural Suspense as he tries to figure out exactly what's going on.

Is he losing his mind?

Or does everything that is happening have a deeper meaning?

Check it out here: December 21st: An Urban Supernatural Suspense

Where. Is. Haseem?! A Romantic-Suspense Comedy

Ever been ghosted??

Well, Stephanie has, and it doesn't feel good.

After a series of mishaps in the love department, Stephanie meets Haseem. They seem to hit it off and the chemistry between them is steadily building. Until...

Haseem disappears.

Where did he go??
No one seems to know.
But Stephanie is determined to find out.

Follow this story of romance, suspense, and comedy as Stephanie tries to figure out how the man of her dreams could just vanish without a trace.

Check it out here: Where. Is. Haseem?! A Romantic-Suspense Comedy

Tanisha Stewart's Thrillers

The Quiet Ones Series

Should Have Thought Twice: A Psychological Thriller

Fooled Me Once: A Psychological Thriller

Never Saw Me Coming: A Psychological Thriller

Reap What You Sow: A Psychological Thriller

Surprise Surprise: A Psychological Thriller

The Enemy You Know: A Psychological Thriller

The Love Conquers All Series

A Praying Wife vs A Preying Woman

A Praying Husband Versus A Preying Man

The Red Series

The Deadbeat: A Psychological Thriller

The Student: A Psychological Thriller

The Patient: A Psychological Thriller

The Bridesmaid: A Psychological Thriller

The Hitchhiker: A Psychological Thriller

The Babysitter: A Psychological Thriller

The Neighbor: A Psychological Thriller

The Trainer: A Psychological Thriller

Standalones

Where. Is. Haseem?! A Romantic-Suspense Comedy

Caught Up With The 'Rona: An Urban Sci-Fi Thriller

December 21st: An Urban Supernatural Suspense

Everybody Ain't Your Friend: An Urban Romance Thriller

The Maintenance Man: A Twisted Urban Love Triangle Thriller

Not What It Seems: A Christian Romance Thriller

Vengeance Is Mine: A Psychological Thriller
Clean Up Woman
The Governor's Wife
Wrath (7 Deadly Sins Series)
Long Way Home